THE BALLOON PEOPLE

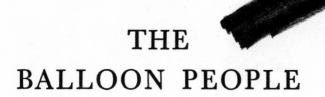

THE
BALLOON PEOPLE

ANN STONE

Illustrated by Philip Gough

McGRAW-HILL BOOK COMPANY
NEW YORK ST. LOUIS SAN FRANCISCO

FOR RUTH

Library of Congress Cataloging in Publication Data

Stone, Ann.
  The balloon people.

  SUMMARY: Ben and his sister help the good Balloon
people against their enemies.
  [1. Fantasy. 2. Balloons—Fiction] I. Gough
Philip, illus. II. Title.
PZ7.S87593Bal [Fic]   74–9703
ISBN 0–07–061687–6 (lib. bdg.)

Printed in Great Britain by
REDWOOD BURN LIMITED
Trowbridge & Esher

First Distribution in the United States of America
by McGraw-Hill Inc., 1974.

CONTENTS

Chapter 1

A FLYING VISIT

ONCE there was a family of three children called Ben, Miranda and Daniel. Daniel was only a baby when this story begins, so he doesn't play a great part in what happened one summer in the village of Langleymere, where they all lived. Their house was on the outskirts of Langleymere, which was a large village, and behind it was a steep hill, covered with trees at the top. Beyond the hill were the shores of Langleymere Lake, where they often went swimming and boating in the summer.

One day, the first really hot day of summer, Ben quickly closed his bedroom door and crept quietly down the stairs, carrying a rolled-up towel under his arm. (I should say that Ben's idea of quietness was often not the same as other people's, for he was a tall boy, with large feet, and was often known as Big Ben, on that account.) Before he had reached the bottom, Miranda's door opened.

"Where are you going?"

How suspicious she sounds, thought Ben. "Oh— just out." He tried to be casual.

"Are you going swimming then?" (She had seen the towel.) "Wait—I'll come with you!"

Ben sighed. Then he said firmly, "I'm going by myself today. I'll go with you tomorrow if you like."

"It'll be raining by then," she said sulkily, but she went back into her room, apparently satisfied.

Ben made his way quickly up the steep path to the top of the hill, disappearing into the trees. He glanced behind him once or twice, as though to make sure no one was following. He felt slightly guilty about deceiving Miranda, for he meant to go, not to the lake, but to a place she didn't even know about, his own private camp.

In any case, I'll go swimming afterwards, he said to himself. Somehow, he didn't want to tell his sister about the camp—not just yet.

He soon reached a clearing, where a rough track ran down the other side of the hill to join the main road. In the clearing was his camp. Ben always thought of it as a tower, but it was really only what was left of a circular stone building. He didn't know when it had been built, nor what it had been used for, nor who had lived there, but he always imagined it had once possessed battlements, like a castle; if so, they had crumbled long ago. The walls were thick and low enough to see over the top, except at the entrance, which was a stone archway. Inside there was a circle of fine, short grass, perfect for picnics or camping. Part of the way round it ran a ditch, which Ben always thought of as a moat, and which sometimes filled with puddles when it rained. Of course it was not deep enough for a moat, and there was no

8

drawbridge, only a few paving-stones in front of the archway, but the ditch did give the place the look of a fort, or a castle. Ben had never met anyone else here—he supposed they couldn't be bothered to climb the hill.

He lay inside the stone circle on the short grass, looking up at the blue sky and thinking of a program about a balloon race that he had seen on television the day before. There was something about balloons that appealed to Ben, though he couldn't

9

have explained it; he had always wanted to go up in one.

He imagined a balloon of his own as he lay there, looking up into that clear sky. It would be red, with gold bands, and would have a large basket to sit in. He knew just how to make it work—you threw out sandbags to make it lighter, so that it would rise, and you dropped a heavy rope to trail on the ground, which brought you down. How glorious it would be to sail high above the ground, with a box of sandwiches and a map of course, and . . . Ben sighed, thinking, What's the use of planning an expedition that is never going to happen? The sun beat down on the tower. The grass was tickling his ears, but he liked the feeling and didn't move. A fly tickled his nose. Insects hummed.

A few minutes later—*was* it only a few minutes?— Ben heard faintly, as though in a dream, a creaking noise. He was so drowsy that he could only open his eyes in slits. I must be dreaming, he thought. It can't be true. Instead of the circle of blue sky above him, there was a dark shape, with ropes. It was swaying like a ship and creaking like a basket chair they had at home. Through the ropes he glimpsed a flash of red and gold, lit up by the sun. The groaning of the ropes and the creaking noise grew louder. "Look out!" cried a voice. "Land ahoy!"

Ben rolled rapidly towards the stone walls. A thud followed and then a louder grating noise. These, he later found out, were the landing-rope hitting the ground and the basket itself. The sky was dark with balloon material, billowing untidily and flapping as the gas inside escaped, hissing. Even though he was a brave boy, big enough to hold his own against anyone, Ben was a little awestruck. The balloon had come to rest inside his tower; there was only just enough room for them both.

Over the edge of the balloon basket appeared a telescope. A hand brandished it vigorously. Then a small, whiskered face showed itself. It was a cat, a tabby cat with a chalk-white shirt front. On its head was a peaked yachting cap and tears were streaming down its furry face.

"Poor pussy!" cried Ben, too concerned to be much astonished. "Whatever is the matter?"

"Pushkin, you foolish animal," said a voice gruffly, from the depths of the basket, "why must you choose this particular moment to peel the onions?" The hand and telescope inch by inch became a shoulder and a red face and a bowler hat. Mr. Perkins had been thrown to the floor of the basket when the balloon landed and now rose to his feet, hampered by a stiff black suit and a high, starched collar. He was, not surprisingly, sweating in the hot sun.

"So hot, so hot," he muttered, "and an annoying obstruction in the landing station too." He glowered at Ben, his black eyebrows meeting.

"I'm *not* an obstruction," said Ben, ready for an argument, "and in any case——"

Mr. Perkins interrupted. "Now you're here, boy,

you may as well help." Suddenly he smiled, and Ben forgot his crossness immediately. Mr. Perkins looked altogether different when he smiled.

The pair of them had now climbed out of the basket, and Ben saw that the cat was indeed carrying a plate of onions. "For soup," he explained, yawning. Ben was to think for a long time that Pushkin was bored with the whole world, as he was always yawning, and even spoke in a yawn, but he later discovered that this was just his way, and he was really alert and noticing everything. Many people were deceived by him.

Mr. Perkins began darting about the grass, coiling ropes, unpacking provisions, and folding the balloon, so that it was out of the way. Ben couldn't help seeing that the ropes were becoming more tangled, the provisions disordered and the balloon like a badly packed parcel. As Mr. Perkins worked, he addressed Ben in spurts; Ben didn't catch all he said by any means.

"Perkins and Pushkin the names ... Perkinpush for people in a hurry . . . always in a hurry . . . have to be efficient . . . Push inclined to be slack . . . need a new crew member . . . you'll do as well as another, I suppose." He finally tripped over a rope and was silent for a moment while he undid it.

"Such a bore," said Pushkin languidly. Reclining on one paw, so it seemed, he was juggling with lightning speed with a primus stove, a saucepan, a box of matches and some packets wrapped in greaseproof paper. Ben blinked, for in a flash a check tablecloth was spread on the grass with bacon and eggs cooked to a turn, steaming onion soup and bread and butter. Miraculously the balloon was quite in order, too.

Mr. Perkins sat down to the meal with a sigh of satisfaction. "All shipshape at last," he said. "Though goodness knows I've had to slave to finish in time. What can you expect with such an idle cat for a mate?" As he made the last remark, he gave Pushkin an affectionate smile.

Pushkin showed all his back teeth in a big yawn and stared at Mr. Perkins with round green eyes. Anyone could see that the cat was very fond of him.

"So good for keeping out the cold," said Mr. Perkins to Ben. "Onion soup, I mean."

It crossed Ben's mind that this was a rather odd remark to make, since the temperature was at least eighty degrees, but instead of questioning it, Ben began to eat, and a delicious meal it was, too. Somehow it didn't seem at all strange, to be eating out there on the grass, leaning comfortably up against the big basket. They hadn't even asked his name, yet they seemed to accept him as one of themselves. All thoughts of home had vanished from his mind and he looked forward eagerly to his first balloon flight with his new, fascinating friends.

Chapter 2

PUSHKIN, PERKINS AND PASSENGERS

THE three balloonists drank the last of the steaming cups of cocoa, which ended their meal. Strangely, this made Ben feel cooler, and not hotter, as you might expect. He discovered later that the Balloon People always ate unusual mixtures of food, and never matched their food to the weather or the season, as most people do. On a cold day, they might have strawberry ice cream garnished with frozen shrimps—warming and delicious, by the way—or another time it would be a mixture of scrambled eggs and apricot jam, or apple pie served with pea-soup sauce. During the whole time that Ben was with the Balloon People, he always found their meals delightfully surprising, and never once felt sick, as he might have done at home.

"Time to board balloon!" cried Mr. Perkins, taking the lead as usual, and consulting his watch. "It's fifteen hours precisely—stir yourselves, you lazy lubbers! Man the guns!"

Ben could see no guns, but he dutifully began to collect dishes and put them in a picnic basket, wanting to show how helpful he could be. Mr. Perkins was emptying the balloon basket almost as quickly as it was being loaded, but by working so fast that he was just a furry blur, Pushkin managed to finish the job. Ben was so dizzy by this time, especially after such a large meal, that he thought he must be imagining things when he saw a boy's red tie fluttering round the corner of the basket. The worrying thought that someone might have followed him to the tower was still at the back of his mind, so he peered round the corner. Of course, there was nothing there—it must have been an effect of the dazzling sun.

Pushkin jumped smartly into the basket, and Ben climbed in more slowly, thinking that it was just like a bigger version of the laundry basket at home. It was full of other baskets, large and small; Ben had never before seen so many baskets in one place. It was quite difficult, in fact, to find a comfortable place to stand.

"Is there a cat basket too?" he asked Pushkin, trying to make pleasant conversation.

"A *what*?" Pushkin's neck fur rose and his tail swelled twice its size, into a stiff brush.

"Sorry, Pushkin," said Ben cheerfully, realizing at once that he had made a mistake. "Of course you're not that kind of cat."

Pushkin allowed Ben to smooth his hurt feelings, but for a moment he had looked very fierce indeed. I wouldn't like to face *him* in a fight, thought Ben.

Pushkin then let down to the ground a basketwork

15

gangway and took out a bamboo pipe. "Piping you aboard now, sir," he said respectfully to Mr. Perkins. Ben had seen this ceremony before, on television; then it had been on a ship, not a balloon. He held his breath as Mr. Perkins wobbled uncertainly up the rickety gangway, his stiff white collar nearly choking him. In one hand he carried the telescope and in the other, a rolled umbrella—Ben never saw the umbrella opened during the whole time he knew the balloonists, rain or shine. Sometimes he thought it was made of solid plastic.

The great moment had come at last; there was nothing left to do but take off. Ben drew himself up to his full height, which made him taller than either of the others. He did this partly from excitement, but partly, it must be confessed, from fright. After all, it's no small thing to make one's first balloon flight and Ben hadn't noticed any parachutes.

"Are we off now?" he whispered to Pushkin.

"Of course not," replied the cat, yawning. He pointed upwards to the empty sky and then downwards to the limp, sad heap of red-and-gold balloon material. "He always forgets—expects the birds to carry us up, or something."

"Oh yes," said Ben, trying to sound knowledgeable. "Hot air to fill the balloon."

"Not hot," said the patient Pushkin, "nor air. Hydrogen gas."

Then Ben remembered seeing the television balloons being filled from long cylinders, through a pipe. There on the grass were their own supplies of gas, which must have come in the basket. In a short time, Pushkin had emptied them all into the balloon, so that it billowed into the air, shining and beautiful. The basket gave a slight lift, as though it couldn't wait to be free.

As the balloon rose, Ben's stomach gave a downward lurch, as though half of him were being left behind. He could almost touch the rough stone walls of the tower, and a short distance away was the huge trunk of an oak tree. As he was so tall, he could easily see over the basket's edge, so he leaned out eagerly. At intervals, from a heap on the floor of the basket, Pushkin emptied a sandbag over the side. The sand sprayed towards the ground, and the heap of sandbags grew gradually smaller as the balloon rose higher.

"The cock is crowing west," miaouwed Pushkin softly.

Whatever can he mean? thought Ben, puzzled, and then caught sight of the weathercock on the village church tower. Now he remembered: balloons were blown by the wind, so you had to wait until it was in the right direction. He noticed that all this time Mr. Perkins was huddled in a corner of the basket, his hands covering his face and his bowler hat tipped forward. Someone wasn't ashamed to show he was frightened; poor Mr. Perkins, he had never got used to the takeoffs.

"Fasten your seat belts, please," he said with

17

authority, the words muffled by his fingers. As there were no seat belts, no one moved.

There were only a few sandbags left now. "Look, someone has left a toy car behind on the grass!" cried Ben. "And it's moving too—what an accurate model!" He grew enthusiastic, as collecting car miniatures was one of his hobbies.

"What a *tremendous* bore," drawled Pushkin. "How *un*observant you boys are."

Mr. Perkins rattled away, still through his fingers: "For your information, gentlemen . . . may unfasten seat belts . . . your captain for this flight is Perkinpush . . . now flying at an altitude of fifteen hundred feet . . . at five miles an hour . . . hope enjoy flight, thank you . . . have-a-barley-sugar-Big-Ben." Breathlessly he thrust a sweet into Ben's hand and sucked one himself noisily.

Ben was blushing now, because, of course, the model car was a real one, running on the main road near the tower; the mighty oak was a green blob among many others and the tower a small grey ring; his village looked like a toy one he had at home, with toy cows and sheep in the fields around. He clutched the side of the big, swaying basket, which creaked in a familiar way—he could almost be sitting in a basket chair they had at home. He felt like a lord, floating under this beautiful gold and red bubble in the sunlight, with only the sound of the breeze and the birds. He forgot his home. In other words, he began to enjoy himself.

The balloon was still rising slightly and Ben found that sucking the barley-sugar stopped the faint buzzing in his ears. He had heard that people sometimes took them on plane flights. "You've certainly thought of everything," he said aloud.

"Natur-rr-ally," purred Pushkin. "Now we've embarked, I'll show you around."

He sprang lightly into the center of the basket, then suddenly stiffened, and a ridge of fur stood up stiffly along his back. "What's this-ss?" he hissed, pouncing nimbly upon a piece of material poking out from a canvas at the bottom of the basket. Ben recognized it in a flash as the red tie he had seen, or imagined he had seen, before they left the ground. Pushkin jumped hard on the canvas with an ear-splitting screech—even Mr. Perkins gave a start.

A scarlet face promptly emerged from underneath. The material was not a red tie but a red hair-ribbon. "Miranda!" cried Ben. The three balloonists were so agitated that the basket lurched in the most dangerous way.

"And why shouldn't I come too and join in the fun? No need to have jumped on me so hard, by the way," she added, wriggling out completely. "I thought it was rather clever of me to hide from the three of you."

"Miranda, you are the most conceited——" began Ben.

"Most irregular, most irregular," said Mr. Perkins, looking her up and down, his black eyebrows meeting. "What have we here? A girl, it seems."

"Ir-rr-egular . . . a gir-rr-l," growled Pushkin. He was really more annoyed at having missed her in the first place than because she was there.

"I didn't mean to offend you, dear Pushkin," said Miranda, with her most winning smile, "but it was the only way I could come, and now I'm here, please let me stay."

"It's my sister," said Ben. "She must have followed me."

"If she managed to get into our balloon without being seen," said Pushkin, "then she must be very clever indeed. I think she will make a good balloonist."

"Strictly speaking," said Mr. Perkins, flourishing his umbrella, "she's a stowaway. But I may agree to overlook . . ."

"That's settled then," interrupted Pushkin. "Miranda stays. What can you do, Miranda?"

She was taking great gulps of air and looking down at the ground with interest. She wasn't a bit alarmed, though they were floating along at a steady speed and were already far away from home.

"Well," she replied, "I can run fast, and quietly, and I'm very good at disguises, of course."

"Prove it." Pushkin stood with his paws on his hips.

"Turn your backs then."

When they turned around again, they all gasped with surprise. (Except Ben, who had seen it all before, though her tricks still had power to astonish him.) Where a fair-haired plump little girl had stood before, there was now a bent old man, bald and with spectacles.

"Easy," said Miranda, pulling off the rubber skullcap and spectacles and standing up straight. "I always carry a few disguises with me. I can do voices, too."

"I'm sur-re you can," purred Pushkin, impressed. (Perhaps I should say here that although Miranda had so far seemed to be altogether an over-clever and superior girl, Ben and others who knew her well, could have told you that she was not, as later happenings in this story will show.) At any event, she was now definitely accepted as one of the party, and while Mr. Perkins kept watch over the progress of the balloon, Pushkin showed Miranda and Ben its equipment.

All around the inside of the basket hung dozens of small objects on bamboo pegs. Some that the children noticed were:

> maps
> a bamboo telescope
> toothbrushes
> a can opener with a bamboo handle
> coat hangers holding a change of clothes
> a mirror in a bamboo frame
> two photographs, one of Pushkin (smiling)

and one of Mr. Perkins (serious), each standing by a balloon.

"This is a barometer, isn't it?" said Ben, pointing.

"Yes," said Pushkin. "It gives us some idea of what the weather will be like. At the moment it's pointing to fair. It always is, of course," he added. "It's been like that since we bought it."

Miranda and Ben looked puzzled.

"Then how can you tell when it's *not* fair weather?" asked Miranda.

Pushkin looked at her pityingly. "You've got eyes, haven't you?" he said rudely. "Really, it's amazing how unobservant people are. Now *this* is a thermometer. We never allow it to sink to freezing point."

"What happens when the weather's freezing, then?" asked Ben.

"We're never here."

What can he mean? thought Ben, puzzled. But one look at Pushkin's face showed him that the cat was not willing to tell them more about the thermometer.

"Drop that subject, please," ordered Mr. Perkins, without turning around.

"This is our altimeter," Pushkin continued hurriedly. "It tells us how high up we are. Very useful, especially in a fog, when we can't see the ground, though we don't have many of those in the summer."

"What about the winter then?" asked Miranda. "We had one that lasted nearly a week last Christmas, do you remember?"

Pushkin looked away, and again the children had the impression that this was a forbidden subject.

"Not yet, not yet," said Mr. Perkins.

Pushkin opened one of the baskets and took out a plate rack. He found the dishes they had used for their meal and put them in. "For washing and drying dishes," he told them. Hoisting up one of the long bamboo poles that were lying at the bottom of the basket, he suspended the rack in the air.

"I see!" cried Ben. "The rain will wash them and the wind will dry them—what a good idea!" He hated washing up.

Pushkin then pegged a line of washing, taken from another basket, to another pole and fixed that too onto the balloon basket. Now the balloon looked more than ever like a ship at sea. "Not too many clothes at once," said the cat, "or they'll act like sails and we'll be blown along too fast."

The canvas that Miranda had hidden under turned out to be a collapsible bath, which could be suspended under the balloon and filled with rain-water. Each of the small baskets held something interesting—collapsible plates and cups, for instance, collapsible bicycles—"In case we don't land exactly in the right place," explained Pushkin—a tent, sleeping bags, collapsible buckets and knives and forks like telescopes. In fact nearly everything in the balloon could be folded into an incredibly small space. Ben and Miranda were full of admiration.

"You've got everything anyone would need," said Miranda.

"Pre-recisely," said Pushkin smugly. "We have to, you know, in case They get us in a fix."

"They?" said Ben, inquiringly. But Pushkin only yawned, instead of replying.

"What's in here?" asked Ben, looking, without being invited, into a canvas bag fixed to the side of the basket.

"Don't s-snatch!" hissed the cat.

"May as well let them see," said Mr. Perkins, adjusting his bowler in an embarrassed way.

"Very well—they're guns, if you must know," said Pushkin sulkily. Ben then remembered Mr. Perkins mentioning guns when they had embarked.

"Ink guns, of course, and water pistols—need them while They're around."

Again this reference to the mysterious "They." The guns were put away and Miranda admired the basketwork windowboxes containing a gay display of pansies and mustard and cress. Tied to a pole was a wind sock, like the ones you see at the airport, to show wind direction. Altogether, the balloon was a strange mixture—a cross between a house and a ship, or a plane and a camp.

"They've seen enough," said Mr. Perkins, "and in any case, we shall soon be there."

"What is our course, then?" inquired Ben, trying to be balloonmanlike.

"Circular."

Indeed it was. The wind must have changed, because the children leaned out to see the winding road leading into their familiar village, the school, the church with its weathercock (now pointing east), the hill with the tower and then the tower itself, pink in the setting sun. This reminded the children for the first time how late it must be, and of their mother waiting for them at home. They drifted closer, until the basket brushed the topmost leaves of the oak tree.

Mr. Perkins and Pushkin were again transformed into a busy team, rushing hither and thither, letting out the gas in the balloon by pulling a brightly colored rope, dropping the heavy trail-rope which landed the balloon safely, and at the same time, hoisting in the washing and watering the flowers from a basketwork watering can. (However does it hold water? thought Ben.)

With a dull thud, the balloon hit the ground, plumb in the center of the tower, as before. Mr. Perkins was now on the floor, hiding, as they had grown to expect. Pushkin was yawning, for what reason they couldn't tell.

"Thank you very much," said Ben, "for the flight, I mean. . . ." He was stammering, not knowing quite what to say. He wanted to say, "Will you take us on another flight?" but somehow the words wouldn't come out.

25

Pushkin held out a limp paw to each of them, in a dismissing kind of way. "Not stopping," he said, helping them out of the balloon.

"What shall we tell our mother?" asked Miranda. It was now dreadfully late, long past their bedtime.

"Up to you," said the unhelpful Push. "But remember, people are *so* unobser-rr-vant."

"But aren't you coming back?" Ben was quite bewildered.

"It's going to rain for the next few days," said Mr. Perkins, as though this were an answer.

The cat prepared to leave. He had filled the used sandbags from a heap of sand outside the tower, which the children hadn't noticed before, and was piling them in the basket, ready to be emptied again. He spent a little time filling the balloon from some more gas cylinders in the bottom of the basket. The number of things in that basket was really amazing.

By the time they were ready to go, only the top of Mr. Perkins's bowler hat showed above the basket. And as the balloon rose, soft miaouwing words floated down through the dusk. "Never-r think about the futur-re, only the pr-resent!"

Too full of their own thoughts to speak, the children watched the last glimpse of red and gold disappear into the distance and then hurried home through the darkness.

"Hello," their mother greeted them cheerfully. "Ready for supper?"

They ate hard-boiled eggs and salad—how dull, after the balloonists' food—and went quietly to bed.

Nothing would ever be the same again.

Chapter 3

A FARM IN THE HILLS

THE rain spouted from the eaves above Ben's bedroom window, hitting the soaked earth below with a slapping sound. The dreaming Ben heard a balloon basket fall to the ground and sat up in bed, smiling. It was a moment before he realized that this was yet another wet day, and there was no balloon. His smile vanished and the corners of his mouth turned down. He sighed. It had rained every day since their ride with Mr. Perkins and Pushkin.

At breakfast, he and Miranda looked miserably at each other over their cornflakes. Only baby Daniel, humming and spooning sticky cereal into his mouth and hair alternately, was in the room, so they could speak freely.

"I'd never have thought," said Miranda, in what Ben privately called her "whiney" voice, "they'd have just gone off like that."

"After all, they didn't say anything about coming back," said Ben reasonably, but feeling wretched inside.

"You don't care, that's what it is." Miranda's voice became high-pitched and accusing.

"I do!"

Daniel saw that this was going to develop into one of those ding-dong "Yes, I do," "No, you don't" arguments, which have no real conclusion. He slurped deliberately into his milk, knowing his mother wasn't there to stop him, and gazed out of the window in search of something more interesting. "Napple," he said. "Fell. Wheeee!"

"Dan wants his diaper changed—I'll fetch Mother," said Miranda, getting up.

Then Ben looked out of the window, too. On the flowerbed outside was a round, red—*balloon*. It was only a few inches tall. Ben blinked crossly.

"Napple," said Daniel.

Ben opened the French window stealthily, as though he expected the object to scuttle away. "It *is* a balloon, not an apple, Dan!" he cried, his voice squeaky with joy. "Dan, Miranda, it's a tiny balloon! They haven't forgotten us—I knew they wouldn't." He was holding it now; a red balloon patterned with diamonds lay in his hand; the basket, a strawberry punnet, held a posy of pansies tied to a note. Miranda and Ben read, in minute handwriting, "Rain at seven, fine by eleven."

Then the two children noticed something else: the rain had stopped and a watery sun was shining into their excited faces.

Up at the tower, they heard the church clock strike eleven. On the last stroke, sure enough, the longed-for shape drifted into sight. Within minutes it had landed. Both children were smiling, delighted at having interpreted the message correctly.

Miranda opened her mouth at that point—Ben knew it was only to complain, so he gave her a little warning nudge and waved eagerly to Pushkin, who was leaning over the side of the basket. They could hear Mr. Perkins at the bottom, moaning, "I wish I hadn't come, I *do* wish I hadn't!"

Miranda shut her mouth again—even she realized that it wasn't wise to grumble at the delay in the balloon's return. Pushkin was lowering the gangway and greeted them casually, as though he had left them only five minutes ago. "Hello, Big Ben, Miranda! Have a cabbage sandwich." The children

ate while he was preparing to set off again, which didn't take long, for this time he had touched down by using the trail-rope alone, and had not let the gas out. Ben stopped to tie the laces of his big walking boots more securely. It had seemed a good idea to bring them, but now he was finding them rather heavy for such a fine day. Miranda was wearing sandals.

They didn't dare ask where they were going. "I expect it'll be a little round trip, like last time," whispered Miranda.

Mr. Perkins's face was green, and this time he didn't get up from the floor of the basket at all. He was huddled in a heap, but his suit was still pressed into beautiful stiff creases and his snowy collar was starched and rigid under his chin. He nodded briefly to the children.

The basket rocked and slowly left the ground, bumping clumsily against one of the tower walls as it rose. "Mind your step, Push—not a very good takeoff," muttered Mr. Perkins, his black eyebrows twitching. Poor Pushkin was, as usual, doing all the work and taking all the blame.

The ascent was as thrilling as before. The great sweep of open country, dwarf trees, houses and cars tilted suddenly as a wind current caught one side of the balloon; they all drew in their breaths sharply, but the basket was already swinging again onto an even course. "The cock is crowing southwest," sang Pushkin triumphantly, adjusting his peaked cap, which had been knocked askew by the lurch of the balloon; he gazed at the sun for a moment, purring to himself and seeming to forget everyone else. Ben and Miranda were leaning far over the basket's edge, quite undismayed by the dizzy drop beneath them. Already they were over unfamiliar country, carried fast by a strong wind, and in the distance they could see the glittering spires and weathercocks of a large town.

Pushkin spread out his map and showed the children where they were. The town, to the children's interest, turned out to be called St. Alfred's, which was where their father worked, and they searched the streets excitedly for his figure, among the scurrying people, small as insects, who thronged them, as the balloon flew directly overhead.

"You sillies," said Mr. Perkins. "How foolish to think you could see him at this height."

"Can they see us, then?" asked Miranda.

"Of cour-rse not," said Pushkin contemptuously. "People never notice *anything*."

"Well," replied Miranda, ready for an argument, "I'm sure *I* would notice a large red and gold balloon any day."

"You think so?" Pushkin looked at her through slit eyes. "Look again."

"Look where?"

"Just look, that's all." Pushkin could be maddening sometimes.

Ben and Miranda stared around them; they saw clouds, a few birds and nothing more.

"Look harder," insisted the cat softly.

The children stared until their eyes bulged. Gradually faint shapes began to appear in the sky. It was as though there had been a thick fog which was now lifting, though actually the sky was clear and blue. In amazement, they made out the forms of other balloons. One was yellow with red stripes, another blue with pink flowers, another crimson, with a pattern of silver birds. They were all sizes and shapes, too, some vast as houses, with baskets made in two

33

stories, others only big enough to hold a single pas-
senger. They saw one balloon pulled by two large
birds and another shaped like a scaly fish. They all
floated peacefully and noiselessly as in a dream, and
as the children watched the sky was all at once thick
with them, glowing in the sun and looking light as
bubbles. Ben and Miranda turned to Pushkin in
astonishment and wonder.

"Look again," was all he said. The balloons had
disappeared, and they saw only their own balloon
above them, and their dark round shadow moving
over the ground below.

"It's too soon yet, Pushkin," said Mr. Perkins, smiling.

"Too soon for what?" asked Ben, bewildered. "Was it some kind of magic?"

"*Magic!* Pooh!" Pushkin almost spat. "All they can say is 'Was it some kind of magic?'" He looked disgusted. "They'll be talking about fairies next."

"Or elves," chimed in Mr. Perkins.

"Or goblins."

"Or witches and warlocks."

Pushkin's mocking tone suddenly changed to a sharp, urgent voice. "Sand, quickly!" The balloon had been losing height during this conversation, and to their horror the children saw that a short distance away some electricity wires were stretched directly across their path, glinting wickedly in the sun.

"Emergency! Down below decks!" shrieked Pushkin.

Mr. Perkins and Pushkin feverishly emptied sandbags. The children crouched terrified on the floor of the basket and felt the balloon rise like a high-speed lift. Then, to their surprise, nothing happened. They lifted their heads to see Mr. Perkins, weak with shock, leaning against the side of the basket. They had cleared the wires.

"What would have—happened—if——?" Ben hardly dared say what he was thinking.

Mr. Perkins looked at them solemnly. "My boy, we balloonists never ask that kind of question."

The children soon forgot their fright. In fact it was

much later before they realized how very dangerous that moment had been. They were soon exclaiming to each other over the view beneath. Beyond St. Alfred's rose some hills, purple with heather, and on the highest points stood large, grey rocks. Soon they were sailing through a thin veil of mist, and when they emerged from the damp, clinging stuff, the bright midday sun lit up a green valley surrounded, by heather-covered hills as far as they could see, and in the center, almost directly beneath them, a grey farmhouse with smoke coming from its chimneys, in a nest of barns and stables. Sheep, looking from the air like balls of cotton wool, grazed on the pastures around. It was a well-kept and friendly homestead.

A group of people who had been haymaking gathered round the farmhouse door. They ran to meet the descending balloon. As they drew nearer, Ben and Miranda saw several children, and a few older people. A round-faced, fair woman, who they later discovered was called Emma, shook them each by the hand with a wide, welcoming smile. Ben noticed that she walked with a springing step, hardly touching the ground.

"We've heard all about you, my dears," Emma said cheerfully. "Come inside by the warm fire."

"But it's so hot!" whispered Miranda to Ben.

"Never mind. Do as they say." Ben had already learned not to question the balloonists too much.

"Meet Leo, my husband," continued Emma, leading them towards the house with bouncing steps.

A tall, almost globe-shaped man, with a shiny bald head and a lively manner, bounded across the grass, seeming to walk on his toes like a portly ballet dancer. He was almost like a balloon himself, about to take off. The children had never seen people so light on their feet. There were crowds of children—it was difficult to see exactly how many—darting here and there. Two who seemed more frisky than the rest, and who were also about their own age, were called Felix and Becky.

As the balloonists danced lightly over the grass, Ben and Miranda following with heavy steps and feeling like elephants, Miranda heard Emma say to Pushkin, her gay face suddenly anxious, "Did you meet Them this time?"

"We may have—it's always hard to tell what's *Their* mischief," said Pushkin shortly, looking meaningly towards the listening children. "Tell you later."

"This is our home," cried Felix, leaping across the threshold in one jump.

Inside, the farmhouse was most surprising. Although from the outside it seemed to have an upper floor and upstairs windows, like an ordinary house, inside, the second floor and the inside walls had been taken away, to make one huge room. From the roof, high in the rafters, hung hammocks, large and small, with curtains round them—to be drawn at night, the children supposed—and rickety bamboo ladders to reach them. There was a simply enormous fire, surrounded by basket chairs, some huge, and one or two for babies. The fire was stacked up high with logs and the flames roared fiercely up the wide chimney, even on such a warm summer's day. There was also a large basketwork table, creaking in a friendly way under the weight of a huge meal. How Miranda stared when she saw the food!

Mr. Perkins scurried here and there, fetching chairs up to the table, falling over his own feet, and giving everyone the wrong-sized chair. He looked stiff, black and sad beside the other brightly dressed, round-faced Balloon People, but they were always kind to him, the children noticed, and treated him with great respect. This was because Mr. Perkins had once helped them when they had been in great trouble. Although he was an ordinary human being, different from them, and had never really felt at home in a balloon, the Balloon People always remembered to be grateful to him. He held a special, honored place among them.

"Sit down, sit down," ordered Mr. Perkins, pointing with his umbrella, so they did, though Miranda's chin barely reached the table, her chair was so low, and Ben's chair was so high that he had almost to bend in two to reach his food.

Years later, when they were grown up, Miranda and Ben tried to describe this first meal with the Balloon People to their own families, but everything was so strange, and there were so many new impressions crowding in at once, that it was hard to remember the details. One thing they both agreed upon, however, was that, until that time, it was the most wonderful meal they had ever eaten. True, the mixtures and dishes may not *sound* attractive and this made it the more difficult later, when they were describing how delicious they were.

"Well," Ben would begin, "we started with curried peanuts in chocolate sauce."

"Followed by crystallized chicken, stuffed with bananas," Miranda would add wistfully.   .

"And I remember the rice with cherries."

"And the spinach bread."

"The coconut cheese."

"Oh, the iced potatoes with elderflower pickles!"

"Followed by steaming cups of carrot tea!" Ben and Miranda would sigh, remembering these marvels, but nobody else ever seemed to appreciate them, even in imagination.

Afterwards, Pushkin said to Felix and Becky, "Show these two around the farm—I want to talk privately to Emma and Leo."

Ben and Miranda were only too glad to escape from the stifling atmosphere of the overheated room into the fresh air. Becky jumped for joy outside the door, hitting her head on the porch roof. She rubbed it ruefully. It was unusual for this to happen, the children discovered afterwards; only the younger balloonists sometimes misjudged heights, until they became more practiced.

"And here is the weather forecast for today," came

a deep voice from immediately above their heads. The two children looked up, startled, but there was nothing to see. "In the southwest," continued the voice, rather hoarsely, "there will be sunny periods with occasional showers. Winds will be light and southerly. Outlook for tomorrow is sunny, warmer than today."

"Whoopeee!" cried Felix. "How I hate the cold and rain!" He skipped two feet into the air. There was a whirring of wings and a dark shape blotted out the sunlight. For a moment Ben and Miranda were frightened, as a large rooster alighted silently beside them.

"This is Cornelius," explained Becky kindly. "He's our weathercock."

"I didn't know that weathercocks were ever real birds," said Miranda, astonished.

"What do-oo you mean? Not a real bird?" Cornelius ruffled his feathers, his splendid green and gold tail glittering in the sun.

"You'll have to make allowances for them, Cornelius. They can't help being so ignorant. We couldn't take a single balloon off the ground without your help, we know that."

Ben and Miranda felt very small; they seemed to know nothing in this strange world.

With a harsh flapping of wings, Cornelius returned to his perch on the roof. "People do-oo have some odd ideas," he crowed.

"The sun's lovely and hot now," cried Becky, skipping along. She flung open the door of a large barn. Inside was a jumble of half-finished balloon baskets and bundles of cane and bamboo leaning against the walls.

"One of our workshops," said Felix, "and here"—he opened another door—"is where the balloons themselves are made." Stacked neatly on tables in the second barn were piles of colored balloon material, and there were several sewing machines lying ready.

"Once a week we go to market," explained Becky, "to buy more balloon materials—cylinders of gas and that kind of thing. We have wool from the sheep to sell, and a few vegetables usually."

"What do you do with the sheep in winter?" asked the practical Miranda. "There must be deep snow on these moors then."

"Winter?" said Felix.

"Snow?" said Becky.

They both looked puzzled, as though they didn't know the meaning of these words.

"Oh!" said Becky. "You mean when we go ____"

Felix immediately put his finger to his lips and changed the subject quickly. "Do you see these thickets here?"

This was the second time that the balloonists had refused to talk about winter. It was certainly odd, but Ben was interested in the trees Felix was showing them, so he said, "They're bamboo, aren't they?

44

I've never seen it growing—in fact, I didn't know it grew in England at all."

"It will, if it's a sheltered place."

They walked across a small bridge over a stream and round clumps of reeds and willow, which provided all the materials for making baskets. There was a winding path through the bamboo grove, and as Felix and Becky turned into it to lead the way, Miranda heard Felix whisper to his sister, "They don't *know* yet, so be careful what you say. They're only here on trial, so far."

Looking at Ben, Miranda saw that he too had heard. She began to feel slightly resentful. Why was there so much mystery about these people? Why didn't they take them into their confidence, and be done with it?

Deep in these thoughts, Miranda and Ben didn't at first notice that the bamboo grove was much bigger than it had seemed, and thicker; the foreign-looking stems curved high above their heads and the air grew chilly; they had almost to run to keep up with the springing steps of the other two, and every so often they lost sight of them altogether, around one of the sharp corners of the path.

The grove grew darker and began to seem more like a forest. Miranda was almost expecting to meet a tiger, and she shivered—yes, it was much colder, too. She tried hard to keep up with the others and lost them ahead, but could hear their faint footsteps through the branches. Suddenly they heard a scuffle, a shriek and Felix's excited voice. "My word! What have we *here*!" There was a shout and then silence. Miranda and Ben turned the corner to see two trembling and terrified old ladies. One was almost throttled by Becky's scarf, and the other was lying on the ground, felled like a tree by Felix's flying tackle.

Chapter 4

TWO DEAR OLD LADIES

FOR a moment, they all stood frozen in different attitudes—Ben and Miranda astonished and indignant, Felix flushed and angry, Becky agitated.

Slowly Becky released her scarf. The poor old lady looked as though she were going to cry. Softhearted Miranda ran up to her. "Are you all right?" she asked anxiously. "Becky, what are you thinking of, frightening her like that?"

Meanwhile Ben had been helping the other one to her feet. "It's none of my business," he began, "but what a rotten thing to do!" He brushed the dried grass from the old lady's coat and said, "Why don't you sit on this log for a moment, till you feel better?"

Miranda's old lady, holding tightly to a bamboo stem, rubbed her eyes pathetically. "Oh dear, I've lost my glasses—can you see them, my child?" Miranda looked around, and found them, rather dusty, but not broken. The old lady took them eagerly from her, put them on with a sigh of relief, and let go of the bamboo stem. Miranda almost exclaimed in surprise as she handed them over. They were so heavy, that she could scarcely lift them, and

47

she wondered how the old lady could bear the weight, especially as she looked so frail. But she said nothing because Ben was busy helping the other old lady by this time.

"Won't you take off that heavy rucksack for a while," he said, "until you've got your breath back, anyway?"

Indeed, she was panting and pale and the rucksack seemed to weigh down her thin back almost to breaking point. Immediately she looked up with piercing, steely eyes, and almost snatched the strap of the rucksack from Ben's hand. "No!" she cried.

Ben drew back, staring.

"No, thank you, young man," she continued more calmly. "It isn't heavy, and I'm almost recovered." She spoke quite normally, so was it Ben's imagination that she had looked, for a moment, a different kind of person?

While this was going on, Becky and Felix were standing apart, rather shamefaced.

"I know you're thinking we behaved badly," said Felix.

"There's quite a simple explanation," began Becky, not giving any.

There was an awkward silence.

One thing, thought Miranda, the old ladies don't seem to hold any grudge against them—*I* would, if it had been me.

Felix and Becky looked at the ground; they obviously felt they were in the wrong.

"Well," said Felix, in the end, "if we can do any-thing at all to help—you see, you gave us such a fright——"

"And we thought——" said Becky, trying to help him out.

"*I* think," burst out Miranda violently, "that you definitely should apologize—as you can't seem to ex-plain yourselves," she added with dignity. The old lady with the glasses reminded her of her grand-mother, whom she loved, so she felt particularly in-dignant at the way the two old people had been treated.

"No need, no need," said Miranda's old lady, looking embarrassed. "We're on a little walking tour, you know." She pointed to her companion's ruck-sack. "We saw this charming farm, and the so delight-ful wood with its sweet little paths. We just couldn't resist a tiny wander inside, could we, Violet?" With her huge spectacles, she looked like an appealing owl.

"Indeed, Lily," answered Violet, "I do think these children are entitled to some explanation." She spoke in a reasonable, dignified manner. "Although their behavior was, to say the least, peculiar. My sister and I," she continued, "were not aware that we were trespassing upon private property. And even if that were so, a polite reminder would have sufficed —we would have departed at once."

Becky dashed forward impulsively. "I'm afraid we made a mistake," she said. "Please come out into the

D

sun, and we'll do all we can to make up for it. Is there anything you would like?"

"A drink of plain water, perhaps," said Lily, looking inquiringly at her sister. "But a shady place would suit us better than sunshine."

Five minutes later, they were all sitting by the stream, Violet and Lily almost hidden under the branches of a weeping willow. Even so, Ben noticed, it was curious how they screwed up their eyes, and turned away from even the weakest ray of sun. He supposed that sometimes old people didn't like strong sunlight.

The two old ladies weren't interested in food, but they seemed to want to chat.

"We saw your darling stream from the hill," said Lily, pointing to the far horizon. "From that rock, as a matter of fact."

"But what a very long way for two old ladies to walk——" Miranda stopped, blushing at her rudeness. She was astonished though. Why, it must be miles away!

"How well kept this whole establishment is, my dears," said Violet, smoothly. "I suppose you take your produce to market sometimes?"

"Yes, on Tuesdays," replied Becky eagerly.

Felix glanced at her, warningly, but she rushed on: "And do come and see our workshops—we've just been showing them to these two."

"So you're from the outside?" asked Violet, turning to Ben and Miranda. "How interesting." Walking after Felix and Becky, she said to them, "And what happens to your sheep *at night*, my dears?"

Felix and Becky were at a loss, anyone could see that.

"Er—I'm not sure," said Felix. "We're usually in bed by then."

"Such obedient little darlings," said Lily, smiling.

Violet and Lily seemed revived by the glasses of water. They allowed the balloon children to show them all over the barns and sheds, and Violet's sharp eyes missed nothing. She asked a great many questions. Lily went out of her way to please the children, praising everything. Miranda and Ben thought she was a dear old thing, even if she were a little gushing in the way she talked.

The old ladies didn't seem in the least tired, and after a while Felix and Becky thought it was time to go back to the house. By this time they were on the outskirts of the farmlands, and it was well past tea-time. They knew this, because they had heard Cornelius crowing four a long time ago. Violet and Lily had produced enormous parasols to protect their delicate old skins from the sun.

"Do come and meet the family, if you want," said Felix hospitably.

"We wouldn't dream of inconveniencing you," said Violet.

"No, no," agreed Lily. "We must be on our way now. It's such a long way home, you know, and our poor old feet might get nasty blisters."

So they parted, and the children made their way towards the farmhouse. They were all weary, and even Felix and Becky were bouncing less than when they had set out. Ben had wished all day that he had worn different shoes—he found the heavy boots awkward and sticky in the hot sun.

As they drew near the farmhouse door, they heard the sound of raised voices, and one that was almost in tears—was it Emma's? Cornelius crowed as they reached the door, and the voices stopped. The children walked in, Ben last, as his feet hurt so much and he was dragging behind.

"Come along now, and have some tea," said Emma cheerfully. "I expect you're——" She stopped, as Ben walked in, clapped her hand to her mouth, and screamed so piercingly that there was an immediate, deathly hush.

"Emma——" began her husband.

"Leo," she cried, her face white and drawn, "look at his *feet*—for goodness sake, his feet!"

The small children who had been playing on the floor, shrank from Ben as though he had a deadly disease, and he was left standing in the open doorway. Emma sank to the ground in a dead faint.

Chapter 5

A QUESTION OF FEET

Everyone looked at Ben's feet, the Balloon People in horror, and Miranda and Ben himself in bewilderment. The balloon children were bunched, terrified, into one corner of the room, and even poor Emma lay neglected until she began to sit up, rubbing her forehead and groaning, like someone waking from a nightmare.

Leo was the first to act. He lifted Emma into a chair, where she sat, her hands dangling limply over the sides. She seemed too shocked to speak.

"Now," said Leo, looking at Ben grimly, "I blame myself for being so careless. Take off those boots at once!" Ben dumbly obeyed, and when the offending boots stood upon the table, the smaller balloon children let out a faint sigh of relief, in chorus.

Leo picked up the boots carefully and examined them with distaste. "It's all right, Emma," he said after a long pause. "These are only ordinary boots." His wife still looked weak and pale. "But it was careless of us not to notice them before, all the same."

"What do you mean?" cried Miranda suddenly, unable to keep quiet any longer. "Ben hasn't done

53

anything wrong! Why are you treating him like a criminal, or something?"

"Father," said Felix, "we *must* tell them."

"Please don't send them away," begged Becky. "We like them so much, and there's nobody else here who's our own age."

"Er—no question of sending them away, or anything like that," replied Leo. "It was just a question of feet, you see. Don't jump to conclusions. But mind, they're still on trial, even if we do tell them a few things." Miranda thought he still sounded suspicious, and poor Ben was looking from one to the other, quite confused.

"Let's all sit down, relax, and have some cocoa," suggested Leo. "Then we can put everything right."

Miranda thought to herself that this would take some doing, but she sat down with the others, all the same, at the long wicker table. She couldn't help noticing that although the others were curious about them, they left a space on either side of Ben and herself, as though they weren't trusted, even yet.

And so it was, as the evening sun shone through the open door on the golden-brown wicker furniture, reflecting points of light in Pushkin's green eyes, as he lay on the hearthrug, and making Mr. Perkins's face glow richly above his somber suit like an autumn apple, that Miranda and Ben first heard the strange story of the lead-footed people and their long rivalry with the Balloon People.

"You see," began Leo, "we didn't notice Ben's

boots, though normally we would have seen them at once. Mr. Perkins and Pushkin had said you were all right, so naturally, we were off our guard."

"And they *were* all right," said Pushkin, flexing his claws. "He certainly didn't have those boots on before."

"No, indeed," said Mr. Perkins, going redder in the face.

"Of course, of course," continued Leo hastily, before an argument should begin. "What I meant to say"—he turned to Ben—"is that for a moment we thought you were one of Them."

"Dear me, dear me," said Emma, going pale again. "I've never had such a shock—and in my own house, too."

"They always wear lead boots, or sometimes shoes," Leo went on. "We call them Lead-Footers." Ben and Miranda still looked puzzled.

"If they didn't," said Becky helpfully, "they wouldn't be able to stay on the ground at all. Gravity, you know," she added.

"How many of these lead-footed people are there, then?" asked Miranda, thinking privately that the whole story was ridiculous.

"Hundreds," said Leo. "A few in every village or town."

"You mean," said Ben, "that in every village there are people who wear lead boots or shoes that hold them to the ground? I'm sure there's nobody like that in our village!"

"They don't wear the lead shoes all the time," said Leo. "Sometimes they take them off, which makes them light enough to rise into the air."

"Like the balloonists, in fact?" said Miranda, not believing a word.

"Yes," Leo agreed seriously, "like us—except they don't need balloons, as they're much lighter than us. And there's one other important difference—*we* go up in the daytime, *they* prefer night." The small balloonists shuddered at this. "They hate the sun," Leo continued, "and of course we can't agree on that point, but as the sky is big enough for everyone——"

"For everyone——" echoed the small children.

"—we were content to live together peacefully until——"

"—they declared war on us," finished Emma, with tears in her eyes.

"For a long time," said Leo, his blue eyes looking into the distance, "we lived happily together. The Lead-Footers went up in the night and, except for an occasional balloon that got lost, we stuck to the daytime. But They weren't content with that. They weren't satisfied."

"Why not?" asked Ben.

"You see, they were always thinking of the future," explained Emma, "which is something we never do. They said we would take up the whole sky."

"And hit their television aerials and spoil their reception."

"And frighten their dogs and cats."

56

"And cause electricity cuts."

"And make it rain more often."

"Or make the sun shine too much."

"Or land in places inconvenient for them."

"Or pour sand in their gardens," finished a small child in the corner.

"We have told them many times," said Leo seriously, "that we shall do none of these things, and that there is plenty of room for all of us. We are very shy and we keep well away from other people. Most people have never noticed us at all. But the Lead-Footers won't listen."

"They want to drive us away."

"Even though we're not in their way."

"They want the whole sky for themselves."

"Even though we're only here in the summer."

"They can't bear to see us enjoying ourselves, that's what *I* think," said the small child in the corner.

Ben and Miranda looked thoughtfully at Leo, who was obviously really upset. The story did seem to be true, after all.

"Where do you go in winter, then?" said Miranda. "We did wonder before."

"I can't tell you that," said Leo. "But we hate the cold—in fact, our children have no idea what winter is."

"Is that why Felix and Becky wouldn't talk about it?" asked Ben.

"And why your thermometers never go down to freezing point?" said Miranda, remembering.

"And why you have roaring fires, even in the hottest weather?"

"That is the reason," Leo nodded.

"What about the balloons we saw on the way here?" asked Miranda. "Why did Mr. Perkins say, 'Not yet,' when they disappeared?"

"You're not quite ready to be one of us yet," said Leo. "That's what Mr. Perkins meant; when you are one of us, then you'll see the other balloons."

Miranda and Ben turned over in their minds what they had been told. "There's one thing that puzzles me," said Ben. "If the Lead-Footers take off their lead shoes to go up, and they're lighter than air—how do they come down?"

"Ah," said Leo. "Now that we *don't* know. So far, they have guarded the secret well. If we did know, it would help us to defend ourselves, but nobody has ever seen them come down."

The whole story of the Lead-Footers began to seem quite unlikely to Ben. "If there are so many of these people around," he said, "how is it that we've never seen or heard of them?"

"They look just like anyone else," Emma assured him. "That is, except for their heavy shoes—they are a sure sign."

"So they go out at night," said Miranda. "Like witches?"

"Magic again," miaouwed Pushkin scornfully. "They'll be talking of giants next, or dragons, or wicked spells."

Ignoring this rude interruption, Emma continued anxiously, "So we have to be most careful who we admit to our little community. Already we have had to arm our balloons——" Miranda remembered the water pistols and the ink guns. Fat lot of use *those* would be, thought Ben. "And we have made ourselves as skilful as possible at navigation, just in case."

"We can never be sure that any misfortune that happens to us isn't *Their* work," said Leo. "I was speaking to Mr. Perkins and Pushkin about your journey here today."

"You mean when we nearly hit the high wires?" said Miranda.

Mr. Perkins shivered. "You can't be sure, you can't be sure," he muttered.

"But how could anyone make you hit a wire if you didn't want to?" objected the practical Miranda.

"It must sound unlikely to you," replied Leo gravely. "I can only assure you that it is so. You must take our word for it. Things are coming to a head here in our balloon family—we hoped you might be able to help. As you know, ina few days' time it will be Midsummer Night, the shortest night of the year, and the height of summer."

"It's always light when we go to bed," said Miranda.

"Yes. Perhaps you've heard of Midsummer madness? In our case we are mad with joy, because it's the longest time in the whole summer that we stay in the air. The night is so short that we don't come down until morning, though usually we don't like night flying. In *Their* case, however, they are mad with hate." On the last word, Pushkin clenched his paws and the balloon children stopped bouncing.

"Why don't you just stay on the ground then, until Midsummer Night is over?" Miranda couldn't imagine what all the fuss was about.

"No!" Leo almost shouted. "That would be giving way—it would be cowardly," he said, quietly but determinedly. "We will fly as much as we usually do, and not provoke them. The sky is for everyone."

"The sky is frr-ee!" cried Pushkin, purring.

"Although it only gets dark for a short time," Leo explained, "they are sure to be out in full force on that night. We must wait and see what happens. Meanwhile, you two may be of some use to us, since you are nearer their world than ours."

"May we, indeed?" said Ben, huffily.

"Afterwards," said Emma kindly, "you may be accepted as one of us, a true balloonist."

By this time darkness was falling, and Emma had lit dozens of large lanterns, which were hanging on long chains from the ceiling. It was as light as day in the farmhouse, and would remain so until morning. The Balloon People were all terribly afraid of the dark. Ben and Miranda were shown two hammocks in a secluded place, and the others, yawning with weariness, went off to bed. Ben and Miranda climbed up their bamboo ladders and lay down in their day clothes. After a short time nothing was stirring in the huge room, and the hammock curtains were all drawn.

Half an hour had passed when Ben gave a little experimental cough, to see if Miranda was awake. She sat up immediately, her hammock swaying dangerously, and whispered, "I'm not asleep either. It's so light in here!"

"I want to talk to you where we won't be overheard," Ben whispered back. "Shall we go outside for a minute?"

It was no easy matter, transferring themselves from the swinging hammocks, rocking like ships on a stormy sea, to the narrow bamboo ladders, and then down to the floor. In the end they reached the ground safely, without disturbing anyone. Perhaps the Balloon People were sleeping more soundly than usual, after the excitement of the afternoon.

Outside, Ben and Miranda sat down by the balloon that had brought them there the previous day, which was now inflated again, ready for the next journey. It was bouncing a little on the grass, trying to escape, but it was held firmly by a strong rope wound around a post. The moon was up, and a lively wind was blowing.

Ben strained his neck, looking up at the roof of the farmhouse. "Just trying to see if Cornelius is asleep," he said. "Yes, I can see he has his head tucked under his wing. Miranda, did you believe all that stuff about the people with lead feet—the Lead-Footers, or whatever they're called?"

"Doesn't it sound ridiculous, when you say it like that," said Miranda at once. "I thought the same— that they're making it all up, I mean."

Neither of the children stopped to remember all the strange things they had believed in, since they first met the Balloon People.

"I didn't like the bit about our being of use to them," said Ben.

"No, nor that whole business about your boots."

"It was mean to make such a mystery of everything."

"And even now they've told us, we can't be certain it's true."

"They don't trust us, that's what it is."

"*And* they think we're stupid!"

"Saying we have to prove we're worth having, or something!"

There was a pause.

"Anyway," said Ben, "the balloon is real enough." He touched the rough basketwork thoughtfully. "But I don't see any sign of the Lead-Footers, do you? They're supposed to come out at night."

"Fancy even expecting to see them!" said Miranda scornfully. "Have you ever seen anybody with lead shoes in our village? Of course not," she continued, not waiting for an answer. "If there had been, we would be sure to know about them." She gazed round defiantly, as though she expected Lead-Footers to rise in crowds from the grassy slopes.

"Perhaps we're not looking properly," said Ben timidly, remembering the dozens of balloons they had seen the day before, though only for a moment. Miranda remembered, too, but she obstinately refused to think about it; once she had got hold of an idea, there was no shifting it, and she was convinced that the whole story about the lead-footed people was a false one. "It must have been done with—er—cameras, or something," she said airily. "Perhaps a sort of mirage, like you get in deserts."

"They did have guns in the basket, though," said Ben, who was always ready to see another person's point of view. "I wonder if there's anything else in there that might prove it, one way or another?"

"Let's have a look, then," cried Miranda, for with her a thing was no sooner said than it was done. She promptly climbed in, and disappeared inside. Ben followed, but more slowly; it didn't seem right to go in without asking—like going into someone else's house, without being invited.

Inside the basket, he felt even more uneasy. "Miranda, I really don't think we ought to interfere. . . ."

"Look," interrupted Miranda, who had found a large pie wrapped in silver paper, "I can't wait to see what's in this!" She seemed to have lost her head completely. Ben made a grab for the pie.

"Miranda, how can you just take it like that? It's not ours——"

"Don't *push*! Can't you see you're rocking the balloon? I almost fell over then."

But Ben had not pushed her; he too almost lost his balance. There was another jerk, and the huge balloon soared upwards like a kite in a gale. Forgetting the pie, they bounded to the side of the basket. Horrified, they found themselves staring, not at the ground, but a barn roof below them, and at the useless trailing end of the snapped rope, which no longer anchored them to the mooring-post.

As they flew up and up, too terrified to try to stop the ascent, the cold greeny-yellow moonlight lit up their two pale, sickly faces. From the shadows, other faces watched their flight, but these were pale with triumph.

Chapter 6

A BALLOON FLIGHT BY MOONLIGHT

WITHIN minutes the balloon had swung high above the moors. The farmhouse, now matchbox size, had never looked more like home to the two frightened children. The cold, black sky seemed to close in upon them. They shivered in the chilly air, and from time to time wisps of low cloud swirled around their heads. A strong wind was up, and the balloon rushed on, soaring upwards as though it had a life of its own. Navigating the balloon had seemed so simple when Pushkin or Mr. Perkins was doing it, but now, in the cold moonlight, the balloon instruments were covered in confusing dark shadows, and even if the children had known how to use these aids, it would have been difficult to find them. All their balloon friends were fast asleep; Ben and Miranda had been careful to leave the house quietly, and not a soul knew where they were.

"I'll throw out some sand," cried Miranda, coming to her senses suddenly.

Before Ben could prevent her, she had thrown out a sandbag, one of the precious few in the basket. Immediately the balloon rose higher. "That makes us go *up*, you idiot!" cried Ben, exasperated. Miranda began to cry.

Ben realized that she was in a panic and said, more gently, "Now we must try to keep our heads—and if you do throw out a sandbag again, remember to *pour* the sand out, and not just throw out the whole thing."

"Why?" asked Miranda.

"Because by the time a heavy bag like that has reached the ground, it'll be falling as fast as a bomb, or a bullet—imagine if it hit someone!"

Miranda looked downcast. What a lot there was to learn. "What's going to hap-p-en to us?" she asked, sobbing.

"I don't know," replied Ben, seriously. He didn't say anything to his sister, but he was thinking of several things that might happen. Supposing, for instance, they were blown right out to sea? They were going fast enough, and the farm wasn't far from the sea, he knew that. No, it didn't even bear thinking about—Miranda couldn't swim well, for one thing. Supposing they hit something? He had no idea where they were, and in any case, it was too dark to see a map—even if he knew how to read a map from a balloon. If they tried to land by releasing the gas, it might be anywhere—perhaps in a tree, or in the middle of a town. So his thoughts ran on. He felt responsible for them both, but had no idea what to do. How angry and upset the Balloon People would be, when they discovered their balloon was missing, and they would never trust them again, once they were found—*if* they were found. Perhaps they would never be found. And then he and Miranda would never be able to explain that it had all been a mistake.

His heart was thumping painfully, and he felt despairing, but he turned to Miranda, who was still crying, and said, as cheerfully as he could, "Soon have you home. Don't worry. Flying a balloon is quite simple—I watched Pushkin and Mr. Perkins, the other times."

Miranda stopped crying and looked more her old self. Ben knew it was a good thing that she had such faith in him, though he felt completely at a loss himself. He leaned over the side to see what he could make out below; the ground was dark, with no lights showing, so he thought they must still be flying over moorland. Perhaps the best thing would be to land now, and wait in the basket until morning, when they could walk to the nearest road, or house.

He began to pick his way through the pile of baskets, with the idea of searching for the rope that released the gas from the balloon. Just then there was a stronger gust of wind and the balloon was swept higher, tipping violently. Both of them were thrown roughly to the floor, Ben scraping his arm on the sharp corner of a basket.

They cried out in fright, and at the same time, lying helplessly in the inky blackness of the basket, which was creaking ominously, as though it were going to fall apart at any moment, they heard a high-pitched whine, growing louder every second. It was an unmistakable noise—a jet airliner. They must have been flying very high for a balloon, because the whole basket became enveloped suddenly in a dense, clammy cloud. Ben expected the plane to loom up and crash into them at any moment. In the darkness, the cold and damp, he had never in his life felt more frightened. He tried to think how often two planes collided in the air—he knew it happened sometimes. He could feel the blood from his scraped arm trickle down, but he didn't bother to wipe it away. As they lay there tensely, the whine grew fainter, and they relaxed.

"It was a plane, wasn't it?" said Miranda, not really expecting a reply.

Was the cloud less dense? Ben peered into it and was rewarded by a glimpse of a watery moon. In a few seconds they sailed into a clear sky. For the moment, at any rate, they were safe.

"Unfasten your safety belts!" said Ben, imitating Mr. Perkins's voice. It was a feeble joke, but Miranda laughed a little. "We *will* get home safely, Miranda, if it's the last thing we do."

"Home?" said Miranda. "Do you mean the farm, or Langleymere?"

For the first time they knew how much they looked upon the farm as home, and they couldn't bear the thought of never seeing their friends again. There was silence while they thought of motherly Emma, and Leo, bouncing along effortlessly, for all his bulk. They thought of Pushkin, always so efficient, and wished heartily that he were there to save them. Even comical Mr. Perkins seemed a tower of strength, looking back. How they missed Felix and Becky— young as they were, they had been brought up with balloons, and would surely have known what to do. Worst of all, they would believe that Ben and Miranda had stolen their balloon, and would never accept them now as true balloonists.

But there was no time to pursue these gloomy thoughts, for they were beginning to lose height, and were again in danger. Down below, a cluster of lights had appeared. "A largeish village, by the look of it," said Ben.

"We're dropping too fast," said Miranda urgently, as the lights grew brighter and they were able to make out the shapes of individual houses. A string of lights stretched out into the distance—the yellow lamps of a main road. Along it moved pinpoints of light, which were cars.

"We can't land here—there's no clear space!" cried Ben. "Quickly, throw out some sand—and *not* the bags as well."

Miranda glanced at him reproachfully, but she took up some bags at once, and began to empty them. It was too late, however. They had misjudged their height, and the balloon swooped and dipped like a bird, low over the village. They heard the sound of voices. In the clear moonlight they could see a party of laughing people who seemed to be returning from some celebration. Ben and Miranda covered their faces, expecting to hit a roof at any moment. Ben thought, Goodness, they'll see us! Then he thought, What does it matter, anyway?

The minutes passed and nothing happened. Gingerly uncovering their eyes, they saw that the balloon had risen again and they had passed over the village. An unexpected gust of wind had lifted it.

The two children watched the village disappear with relief. Poor Ben and Miranda! They would have felt much happier if they had known that they were flying, not over strange country, but over their own village of Langleymere. Their family had been only a short distance away.

"I think we might try to land again," said Ben. "We seem to be over open country again now." Indeed, there were no houses or lights, but they could make out the dark lines of hedges—it was not moorland.

"What if we hit a tree or a fence?" said Miranda in an uncertain voice.

"We'll just have to risk it, that's all," said Ben. "We must have a go—if we wait, it could be even more difficult." As though the balloon were mocking them, at these words, it gave a spurt and a leap. Ben and Miranda clutched the sides of the basket.

"Are you ready?" said Ben, recovering his balance. Whatever happens, he was thinking, we mustn't leave it until we fly over the sea. That would be the very worst thing that could happen. He turned to Miranda. "It's now or never!"

Miranda wasn't listening. "Look, Ben!" she cried. "Water!"

Sure enough, the balloon had been moving faster than they thought, and while they had taken their eyes off the ground, the landscape had changed. Underneath, stretching for almost as far as they could see, lay a grey, watery expanse. The shore was only a faint line already, though nobody could be sure, in the poor light, just how far away it was. The worst has happened, thought Ben, his heart sinking, we're bound to crash.

Miranda's eyes were still fixed on the scene below. It had begun to drizzle, and the cold rain soaked into their clothes. The sky became grey and misty and seemed to merge with the iron-grey water; they were sailing jerkily, blown by wayward gusts of wind, in a dank grey world. Grey sea, grey sky, stretched in every direction.

As the children's hearts sank, the balloon dropped, and the wind died away. They began to fall towards the water.

"Hold on to me, or to the basket, when we hit the water," said Ben desperately. "There's nothing we can do, Miranda."

"Throw out the sand!" cried Miranda.

"It isn't any good," said Ben. "We're bound to fall. There's hardly any wind." It was true. They had lost height considerably, and could almost smell the salt water.

"Never mind, throw out the sand!" Miranda

71

started to empty the sandbags. Mechanically, Ben helped her, wild plans going through his head all the time of swimming for help when they struck the water. Miranda seemed to have a tremendous burst of energy. "Throw out more sand," she urged.

"But it's all gone," panted Ben. "Why bother— you know it's hopeless——"

"*This* can go," gasped Miranda, heaving one of the largest baskets to the side. "Now help me with this one——" She was pulling at another.

"Miranda, you must be going mad!"

"*Help* me——"

Ben started to laugh. After all, what had they to lose? Like crazy creatures, they flung out everything they put their hands on, bottles of wine, blankets, the collapsible bath—"Let the fishes bathe in it," said Miranda, giggling. They hardly expected anything to happen as a result of this, but even in the gloomy light they thought that the water was further away than before.

"Ben!" shouted Miranda, as she hurled out a frying pan. "It can't be the sea—there aren't any waves!" It was true. They had taken it for granted that it must be the sea, but now it began to dawn upon them that this must be a large lake. There were one or two ripples, but Miranda was right—there were no big waves, as you would expect on the sea. What they still hadn't realized was that this was their own familiar Langleymere Lake, where they so often went swimming and boating. Of course, everything looked so different at night.

"Miranda!" Ben was laughing so helplessly, he could hardly speak. "Miranda—look—we're over land now—we've crossed the water. We're safe!"

They collapsed into a heap, shaking with uncontrollable laughter. Ben recovered first. "I suppose," he said, tittering, "we'd better think about landing." He chuckled on the last word. The relief of not finding himself in the sea was too much for him. "Anyway, we can't make tea—we've no kettle," he chortled.

"We can't go to sleep—we've thrown out the p-pillow!" shrieked Miranda.

"No toothbrushes!"

"No bacon and eggs for breakfast!"

"No spoons!"

The two children were beside themselves. It seemed the funniest thing that had ever happened.

Just then there was a loud creak, and the bottom began to fall out of the balloon basket. The basketwork came apart on one side, and the few things still left in the basket began to slide slowly but steadily towards the split. The children stopped laughing. They clung to the side, listening to the tearing and ripping noises, as the whole structure of the basket began to give way. The balloon sailed higher, quite unconcerned. Finding it harder to gain a foothold on the collapsing floor, Miranda clutched wildly at one of the basket's many ropes, just above her head.

There was immediately a hissing noise—the sound of escaping gas. Miranda had unwittingly found the gaily colored rope that Ben had been searching for earlier, which released the gas from the main valve of the balloon. The balloon was going flat as quickly as a punctured bicycle tire.

The two children hung over the side of the basket, holding on for dear life. Just at that moment the moon came into view from behind a cloud, serene and beautiful. It revealed in perfectly clear lines the many rows of high-powered electricity wires immediately in front of them.

The wires came nearer. Ben put his hand upon a heavy coil of rope and threw it out. "Hold tight, Miranda!" he yelled. The rope hit the wires and there was a blinding flash of flame, a sizzling noise as in an instant the rope was burnt up, and a smell of burning fibers. The balloon lobbed awkwardly over the wires and they were deafened by the crunching and crashing of branches and the rattling and clatter of birds, flying up into the air in alarm.

Dead silence followed. They had survived. They had come to rest in a large holly bush.

Chapter 7

FIGURES AROUND A BONFIRE

MIRANDA pulled a holly sprig from her hair. "Ouch!" she said. She felt her arms and legs, but they seemed to be unbroken. Ben was almost standing on his head in the depths of the basket. She tugged at his feet, which were protruding, and his voice came, muffled, "Leave me alone! Do you want to pull my feet off?"

"Nothing much wrong with you," said Miranda.

Gradually, by painful degrees, they extricated themselves from the balloon and then from the bush. Ben noticed that the pansies, by some miracle undamaged, still flourished gaily in their boxes. At length they found themselves in a large cornfield, where the green young corn stretched away before them, looking soft and inviting.

"Let's just lie down here and go to sleep." Miranda's voice was pleading. She began to search for a suitable place.

"No!" Ben took her arm firmly. "Don't you realize that we've no idea where we are, we've crashed the balloon—probably it can never be repaired—and we can't afford to waste time sleeping? We must make some effort to find a house, or at least a road."

Miranda opened her mouth to argue, as usual, but her attention was caught just then by a light in the distance. "There's a house, Ben, and I'm *so* hungry —do let's go there!"

Ben was used to her sudden changes of mind, so he didn't point out that a minute ago she had wanted to lie down in the field.

"I don't like leaving the balloon here," he said, worried, "but I suppose nothing will happen to it— it's too heavy to steal—you'd need a large truck to take it away, and a crane to get it out of the bush in the first place." He thought for a moment. "If we go to the house, they would at least tell us where we are —whether you'll get anything to eat or not, depends on them."

"I do wish I'd eaten that pie, while I had the chance," said Miranda wistfully.

Ben was about to remark that if it hadn't been for the pie they would probably never have embarked upon this disastrous trip anyway, but he knew that it was partly his fault, so he said nothing. What was the use of blaming anyone, now that it had happened?

"We'd better set off for the house straightaway," he said. "I don't know what you want to eat for—you wouldn't be eating if you were at home in bed."

"No, but you don't use up energy when you're sleeping," said Miranda. She was walking off at a brisk pace, in her enthusiastic way. "Come back," called Ben. "I think we'd better look for those col-lapsible bicycles first—we may need them."

"But it's only in the next field," said Miranda crossly. However she came back, grumbling to herself.

Ben climbed around the holly bush. His arms and legs were covered with holly scratches by the time he had discovered the bicycles, which were where he remembered, strapped to the side of the basket. After much straining and effort, he managed to unclip them, and then laboriously force them through the stiff and prickly holly boughs into the open field. As he had never seen it done before, it took him some time to discover how to expand the compact metal objects, small enough to pack into a rucksack, into full-sized bicycles. But he was good with mechanical things, and in a short while he had stretched out the frames, which were closed up like telescopes, opened up the wheels, extended the seat and handlebars and inflated the tire. "How popular these would be, if you could buy them in shops," he said to Miranda admiringly.

They set off on the bicycles along a bumpy field path. Ben led the way, and he could hear Miranda the whole time, behind him, complaining and fussing about how much easier it would have been to walk. At the end of the field they lifted their bicycles over a fence, and Miranda rushed forward eagerly. She stopped, puzzled.

"Why, the house is in the next field."

The house was much further away than they had thought, and in the end even Miranda was glad they had taken the bicycles. Eventually they had crossed several fields and ridden down a lane before they saw the light, a few yards away over a hedge. Then they were close enough to have a good view of it.

It was not a house, but a bonfire.

Miranda spurted forward at once, delighted to see some signs of life again. Obeying some instinct, Ben pulled her back. "Wait——"

"Don't be silly—what's the matter now?" Miranda shook him off impatiently.

"Wait," said Ben again. There was something odd about the flames—what was it? They didn't look cheerful, as bonfires generally do. They were a garish yellow, that was it, instead of being red. He frowned, and took Miranda's hand, drawing her behind the hedge. "Now for once you do what I say," he said. He made her leave her bicycle with his in a ditch, and walk with him along the hedge until they reached a five-barred gate. Through the bars they had a clear view of the whole grassy field. An astonishing scene met their eyes.

In the lurid, yellow light from the flames of this unnatural-looking bonfire several figures were dancing, with curiously clumsy steps. The only sounds were the cracking and spitting of the burning logs and the thudding of the dancing feet upon the smooth turf. Green tongues of flame spurted up among the yellow, and the dancing figures leaped higher with the flames, casting crooked shadows on the ground around the fire. Ben and Miranda stared at each other, round-eyed—this was no innocent garden bonfire.

They shrank back behind the hedge to collect their thoughts.

"Witches!" whispered Miranda.

"Warlocks, too," said Ben. "I'm sure some of them were men."

"And at least two were children."

"Whoever they are, I'm not going near them." Miranda heartily agreed. Many astonishing events had happened during the night, but at least all the others could easily be explained. They sensed that the figures round the bonfire represented something un-usual, and, though the word had not been uttered, evil.

As they watched, the dance seemed to be drawing to some kind of a climax; the figures were bounding higher, but more clumsily, and Miranda, knowing how carefully her father guarded their lawn at home, thought, What deep dents in the grass their feet must be making. Then, as though in answer to an unseen signal, they halted. The group stood motionless in the moonlight, facing the bonfire. Without a word, each put a hand in his pocket and took out a small object, which he raised above his head. These objects glinted in the firelight as they circled above their heads, and seemed to be made of metal. Again, perfectly silently, and all moving together, they replaced the metal objects and bent to touch their toes, as though they were at an exercise class.

"Why," said Ben in amazement, "they're taking off their shoes!"

Miranda gripped his arm tightly and blinked. Well she might, for there was no doubt about it—the figures were *leaving the ground*. Holding themselves stiffly at attention, they floated straight up into the clear sky, as though drawn by threads. Like so many wooden puppets, they dangled, lighter than the air. Some rose faster than others, but soon they were all high in the sky, and then out of sight; their empty shoes stood in pairs on the grass, in a circle round the greeny-yellow bonfire.

"I feel I can breathe properly now," said Miranda, sighing.

"Do you hear that owl?" asked Ben. A hooting noise came from a small wood nearby, sounding strangely reassuring to the two children. At the same time, they heard a whole chorus of small squeaking and snuffling sounds—the field animals, mice, moles, weasels, bats, badgers and hedgehogs were going about their business again. A fox barked in the distance.

"Do you know," said Miranda, "it was *quiet* when we saw those people." She shivered, though the night was warm.

"Except for their feet—I mean, those weren't quiet," said Ben.

They listened, half expecting them to descend again. They had still not fully taken in what they had seen. Straining their ears, they heard, above the natural night noises of the fields, a sharp ringing sound.

"A bicycle bell!" cried Miranda, terrified. She threw herself over the top of the gate, landing heavily on the other side. Ben backed up against the hedge, bracing himself for whatever might happen next. There was silence. Miranda was too frightened to move, and they both waited tensely. Then a drawling voice came from the shadows:

"You r-really ought to be ashamed of yourselves."

With huge, brilliant eyes, Pushkin climbed from the ditch, brushing some loose bits of grass from his fur. And how changed he was! He was crouching close to the ground, his magnificent striped coat blending perfectly with the pattern of shadows, every hair alert, his tail swinging, his satin paws stepping delicately, his emerald eyes glowing brighter than summer leaves—he was the picture of a prowling night animal.

"What a bore, following you two all this way," said the cat. "What an absolute bore!" He yawned.

"Dear, *dear* Pushkin!" cried Miranda, wincing as she got up, for she had bruised herself when she fell. "Please say you're not angry with us, please do! Honestly, it wasn't our fault—at least, not entirely. Do take us home—please." She climbed back over the gate and would have hugged him if he hadn't looked so impressive, she was so glad to see him.

"But how did you know we were here?" Ben wanted to know.

"And, Pushkin," Miranda babbled on, "we saw such a strange sight just now, by that bonfire over there——" She pointed and stopped speaking. The fire was gone. "It *was* there, I'm sure. Ben saw it too— what's happening?"

"Perhaps one day," said Pushkin, maddeningly, "you'll listen to what you're told."

"I know what they were," said Ben, the truth slowly dawning upon him. "Of course, how stupid we were not to guess!"

"The lead-footed people!" exclaimed Miranda. "You mean, we actually saw——?" She broke off in dismay.

"We refused even to believe in them," said Ben, "and now we've actually seen them." It was a sobering thought. Until this moment, neither of the children had remembered the story of the Lead-Footers— because they thought it *was* just a story, in fact, they had dismissed it completely from their minds. "So they weren't witches and warlocks!"

"Humph!" said Pushkin, contemptuously.

"That must be why they danced so clumsily—because of their lead shoes, I mean," said Ben, thinking back.

Pushkin drew himself up to his full height. "Some people carry on as though everything in the garden was lovely." His grass-green eyes stared at them. "Haven't you forgotten something?"

"Please forgive us, Pushkin," said Miranda at once. "We know we've behaved badly and all that.

83

It's just that we're so glad to see you and so many strange things have happened. I know we should have said before that we're sorry."

She really can lay it on thick when she wants to, thought Ben.

"We sailed over some village or other," said Miranda to Pushkin. "And then we came to a lake—do you know, it was so big we thought it was the sea! And we nearly drowned in it too."

Pushkin yawned. "My dear children—don't you know what it was? Didn't you recognize Langley-mere Lake, when you saw it? How very unobser-rr-vant of you."

Ben and Miranda were astounded.

"You mean the village was ours?" said Ben. "My goodness, how far we've come! But however did you find us?"

"Can't go into that now. I'm here, that's all that matters. We must leave here this minute—don't you realize how dangerous it is? Follow me." With no more ado, the cat swiveled around and padded off, leaving them to make their own way as best they could.

As he stumbled after Pushkin, immediately behind Miranda, Ben remembered the crashed balloon. His forehead creased into a worried frown. Whatever will they say when they see what we've done to it? he thought. Miranda was quite cheerful and unconcerned, but he felt sick with misery. He saw that Pushkin had folded up the two bicycles and was carrying them in one paw—he must have picked them up when he rang the bicycle bell. At least, thought Ben, *something* hasn't been wrecked or lost.

That long wearisome trek was one of the unhappiest times of Ben's life. All their narrow escapes from danger that night seemed unimportant, compared with the fact that the Balloon People would never trust them again. We've bungled everything, he thought gloomily, and we didn't even recognize the Lead-Footers when we saw them. He wondered why the balloonists had bothered to fetch them back, and how they had known where to look, but he knew it was no use asking Pushkin in the cat's present mood. So they traveled, trailing their feet and almost too exhausted to go on.

Once Miranda said in a whining voice, "Why can't we ride the bicycles?" Ben could have kicked her.

"Keep to the hedge," said Pushkin, briefly. She had the sense to be quiet after that.

After what seemed hours of walking, but what was actually only twenty minutes or so, they turned a corner, and saw the welcome sight of a large balloon, sitting squarely in the middle of a potato field.

"In you get," ordered Pushkin. "Quiet now, I need to concentrate." The children hadn't made a sound, of course, but they sat in the basket, hardly daring to move in case they offended him. He sniffed the wind, as there was no weathercock in sight, and after a few preparations, they ascended.

85

Ben and Miranda watched him, both thinking the same thoughts. "How easy he makes it look," whispered Ben, admiringly. Indeed, Pushkin's navigation seemed effortless; he casually pulled a rope here, poured some sand there, as though balloon sailing were the simplest thing in the world. At the same time, he was chewing a large lump of cherry cake, giving only half his attention to the balloon. The children were so grateful for being airborne again, and in such skilled hands, that they didn't even mind not being offered any cake. Nor did they think to ask where they were bound for—they felt quite safe.

Chapter 8

LEFT IN CHARGE

AT THE farmhouse door stood a small group of Balloon People, waiting for them. Ben and Miranda could make out a large, round shape, which was Leo, and two smaller shapes, which were probably Felix and Becky. A lump came into Ben's throat as they walked over the dark grass towards the balloonists, and Miranda's heart contracted as she thought of what their friends would say about their escapade. Both children desperately wanted their good opinion, but were afraid they had lost it for good.

Pushkin was greeted with joy by his fellow balloonists. "Thank goodness you're back," said Emma in delight, shivering in the warm night air. "Did you see Them?" She looked anxious.

"Yes, Emma, I did—and so did these two." He waved in the direction of Ben and Miranda.

"Did you now?" said Leo, concerned, springing to Pushkin's side in one leap. "I hope there were no incidents. Did they notice you?"

"Are you quite all right?" Felix asked Ben and Miranda. "We never go out at night, you know."

"No, never!" echoed a small balloon child, who was hanging upon every word.

"Pushkin is so brave," said Becky eagerly, bounding into the air, "but he can see in the dark, so it isn't so bad for him. He's always our night navigator, in an emergency."

Pushkin purred gently to himself and strolled into the farmhouse. He loved to be admired.

"Most dangerous, most dangerous," came Mr. Perkins's voice from inside. "Very foolhardy indeed, my dear Pushkin, to venture out at night, and so near to Midsummer, too. Thought we'd never see you again."

"Oh, r-really, it was nothing," replied Pushkin languidly, yawning.

"Now you two children must be in bed in three minutes flat," said Emma briskly to Miranda and Ben. "And you others too," nodding at Felix and Becky. She chased the small child across the floor. "You little monkey—who said you could get up?"

Thankfully, Ben and Miranda climbed up their bamboo ladders into their friendly hammocks and drew the curtains. Three sleepy cock-a-doodle-doos came from outside.

"I didn't know Cornelius was still awake," whispered Ben. "And who would have thought it was only three in the morning?" It seemed as though several days had passed since they left their hammocks; it was hard to believe that it was only a few hours. They were so tired that in spite of the bright lights in the farmhouse, which easily penetrated the thin curtains, they fell asleep within minutes. Ben's last wak-

ing thought was of the kindness of the Balloon People
—there had been not a word of blame, nor reproach,
and nobody had so much as inquired about the lost
balloon. On the contrary, they had been concerned
only for the children's safety. Miranda's last thought
as she was rocked gently to sleep was, How I wish
I could always sleep in a hammock.

Ben and Miranda woke to the brightness of the morning sun, instead of the lamplight. Looking down, they
could see nobody about, but a faint, croaking voice
could be heard through the doorway: "A fine day is
expected with——" there was a loud yawn "—with
—er—where was I? With an occasional possibility—
I mean a possibility of occasional thunderstorms—or
do I mean sandstorms? Perhaps it's hailstorms——"
There was another yawn, and a cough and a pathetic
sigh.

"Have a little nap, Cornelius." Was it Emma's
voice? "We can do without the forecasts this morning, as it's market day. You'll feel better by the time
we come back."

"Hard on a rooster, these broken nights. How can
I be expected to do-oo my job broberly?" Cornelius
sounded as if he had a cold. There was a sniff and
then silence, so he must have taken Emma's ad-
vice.

Guiltily, the children sat up in their hammocks. It
didn't take them long to get up, as they were still
dressed in their day clothes, and once down the

bamboo ladders, they ventured outside, looking around them nervously.

Leo was there, harnessing a pony and trap.

"I'm afraid we overslept——" began Ben apologetically.

"Oh, there you are," said Leo, cheerfully, turning around. "**Emma will get you some breakfast—but** keep out of her way while she's making it, will you?"

"Come with me," said Pushkin, who seemed to spring out of the ground, he walked so quietly. He motioned them to a secluded spot a few yards away.

"Pushkin," began Ben hesitantly, "I just want to say how sorry we are for everything, and——"

"Look, Big Ben," said Pushkin, "we know you're sorry, and there's no need to say any more about it."

"But what about the balloon?" asked Miranda. "I mean the one we—crashed."

"Someone will pick it up today," said the cat. "No use trying to do it in the dark, was it?"

"But Pushkin," persisted Ben, worried, "I don't think you know how badly we damaged it. The floor is——"

"I saw it," interrupted Pushkin. "Nothing a few repairs won't put right. And don't worry about the things you threw out—nothing else you could do, in the circumstances."

"You mean you *saw us*!" exclaimed Miranda.

"Of cour-rse," said Pushkin, smugly. "I was following you the whole way. And what a business it was, too."

Ben's conscience still pricked him a little. "But aren't you angry with us at all?" Strangely enough, he wanted Pushkin to be angry, though he wouldn't have admitted it; it would have made him feel better, somehow. "Won't you need some of the things we threw out, like the collapsible boat—in the future, I mean?"

Pushkin turned his mysterious green eyes on Ben, scarcely seeing him. "Didn't I tell you before? We never think about the future, only the present."

"What about the past, then?" said Miranda, rather bluntly. "Will you tell us how you found us?" She was longing to know.

Pushkin looked at her pityingly. "You may be fair-rly clever," he began, crushingly, "but you're definitely not clever enough to walk out of that farmhouse, under my very whiskers, without being seen. I should have thought that was plain enough."

"Why didn't you stop us then?" said Miranda, not a bit squashed.

"You were as free as any of us," said Pushkin with dignity. "After the gr-eedy little episode with the pie"—he held up one paw, silencing Miranda's protests—"I could see that the pair-r of you had gone quite cr-r-razy and had interfered with the mooring-rope, so I waited a while, and then set sail behind you. You were so busy quarreling, that you didn't observe me. Most people are so unobser-rr-vant, as I have said before," he added, turning up his nose so far that his cap fell backwards.

91

The children blushed at this unflattering view of their adventures, but they were in no position to contradict it.

"Of course," Pushkin continued, "the wind was wrong, the weather was wrong, the time of day—or night, I should say—was impossibly wrong." He shrugged disdainfully. "But I managed. I landed a short distance away, after you crashed in the mulberry bush——"

"It was holly, as a matter of fact," interrupted Ben, as politely as he could.

"Did its being a holly bush make it a sensible place to be?" said the cat, glaring, his eyes changing color like traffic lights.

"Er—no."

"As I was saying. After these two nitwits had landed in this mulberry bush, what should they do then, but ride off like a couple of moonstruck kittens, right into the middle of a gathering of Lead-Footers!" He paused for effect. "I thought to myself—they may be temporarily deranged, off their heads, but it won't do them any harm to see what we're up against."

"So you knew we didn't believe in the Lead-Footers at first?" cried Miranda.

"Of course," answered Pushkin.

"Isn't there anything we can do, to make up for all the trouble we've caused?" asked Ben.

"In half an hour," Pushkin told them, yawning, "we're all going to market to sell some produce—a cabbage or two. Cornelius usually looks after the farm while we're away, but he was up half the night after seeing you go, and then waiting for us all to come back, so he's gone off duty for a while."

"I thought Cornelius was asleep all the time!" said Miranda.

"You would like us to look after the farm for a whole day?" said Ben. He was overwhelmed at the honor and the responsibility, especially after what he and Miranda had done.

"Just to show that bygones are bygones," said Pushkin, and promptly disappeared.

A delicious smell of bacon frying in rosehip syrup floated from the open door at that moment, so the two hungry children went in.

"Why is your food so different from everyone else's?" Miranda asked Emma, as she helped herself to a codliver cookie. "I don't mean it's not nice," she added hastily, seeing Emma turn in surprise.

"Is it so different?" asked Emma.

"It's absolutely delicious," said Ben, reassuring her quickly, "but it's quite—individual."

"I thought everyone ate this kind of food," was all Emma remarked.

The reason why the balloonists' food was so different, as the children guessed later, was simply that they had never eaten any other meals but their own, so although they started off with the same basic ingredients as other people, they combined them in all kinds of unusual and exciting ways, not realizing how original they were.

Half an hour later, Ben and Miranda stood on the doorstep waving goodbye to a party of gay balloonists, setting off on the long white road that led out of the valley, beyond the hills, to the nearest market town, St. Alfred's. Their round, cheerful faces shone in the morning sun. Leo was singing, and Felix and Becky were bouncing up and down in the back of the pony trap. Waves of joy seemed to flow from the Balloon People as they travelled out of sight. Ben and Miranda watched them go, and then turned back to their duties.

Cornelius was asleep in a chicken house and they were quite alone, in complete charge of the farm. Full of the sense of their responsibility, they resolved to patrol around it, eyes and ears wide open.

"How pleased they'll be when they come back and find how well we've looked after the farm for them," said Miranda proudly.

"Let's see that we *do* look after it well," said Ben, more soberly. "It's only morning yet, and Leo said that they would be back late—they always make a good day of it. They'll go up in the balloons early tomorrow, to make up for lost time."

"Are you afraid of something happening, then?"

"No." Ben didn't sound too certain. "Mr. Perkins said that nothing was going to happen, or he wouldn't have left us in charge. He says the lead-footed people are all getting ready for the grand celebration on Midsummer Night, and if anything happens, it'll be then. Still, I must admit—I'll be glad when they come back this evening."

Then they made a thorough inspection of the farm and outhouses; all was quiet and normal. A few sheep, hot in their woolly coats, lay under the trees. The day passed uneventfully in this way. Soon it was teatime, and still very hot.

"Let's look for a shady place to have our tea," said Ben. "Then we'll have another look around—I mean to do the job properly." He took the packed basket that Emma had left them, and crossed the miniature bridge, making for the bamboo grove.

Miranda was, if the truth were known, bored. Nothing was happening on the farm, and she felt like going to sleep like the animals. "I must say," she said, complainingly, "they hardly needed to leave anyone here. Whatever are we going to do for the rest of the day? I do wish we'd gone to market—it would have been much more fun."

"You're always grumbling, Miranda."

"I'm not the only one! Why don't you——"

"Listen!" Ben broke in sharply. They had reached the fringe of the bamboo grove. Its branches were cool and curving, and its dappled shadows and long pointed leaves were inviting them inside. They both stood still, and heard the sound of voices, coming from some hidden place inside the grove, but not far away, because the conversation was clear enough to be understood.

"So they've all gone off for the day, have they?"

"Yes, with the weeniest pony and cart—they all piled in somehow. I counted them."

"And the two outsiders?"

"We'll never see those infants again!" There was a giggle. "Went up in flames, so I hear—stupid babies. I knew they were bound to crash, after we cut their mooring-rope." The voice was soft but malicious.

"Right. I'm going to report back to headquarters. You may follow shortly."

Ben and Miranda stared wildly at each other. "It's Lily and Violet!" exclaimed Miranda. "I'd know those voices anywhere."

"Surely they must be talking about us?" Ben was flabbergasted. "What was that they said, about cutting our mooring-rope? Then it wasn't an accident," he added unbelievingly.

Miranda seized Ben's arm and pinched him hard, her face lit by a sudden revelation. "Those glasses!" she hissed, ignoring Ben's wince. "They were like shoes!"

"Talk sense, will you?" replied Ben, irritated. The voices had receded and could now only be heard faintly. Violet and Lily must have walked deeper into the grove.

"Lily's glasses—when I picked them up and gave them to her——"

"Well?"

"They were *heavy*, Ben, heavy—as—lead! Don't you see?"

Ben looked blank. "But how can glasses be like feet?"

"And the rucksack—Violet's rucksack," Miranda ran on excitedly. "Don't you remember? When it fell off—she wouldn't let you pick it up?"

"Yes. That did strike me as odd," said Ben slowly.

"And the *sun*." Miranda's voice became squeakier every moment. "They hated the sun! They sat in the shade the whole time—we thought it was because they were old, but it wasn't that at all. Ben— don't you see—Violet and Lily, they're *Them*—or two of them, at least. They're Lead-Footers!"

Chapter 9

LILY IN THE AIR

"So they must have been watching us the whole time when we flew off last night," Miranda was saying. "Thinking we'd never come back, I suppose."

"*And* it was no accident when the rope of our balloon snapped," said Ben. "When you come to think of it, Pushkin or Mr. Perkins would never tie a balloon so insecurely, anyway."

"What I can't understand," said Miranda, "is why Felix and Becky accepted Lily and Violet in the first place."

"If you remember," said Ben, thinking back, "they didn't, at first. You remember how Felix knocked Violet down?"

"Yes, of course. And Becky took hold of Lily."

"Perhaps Felix and Becky had been told to be suspicious of anyone they saw around the farm," said Ben.

"Then they must have been confused because the old ladies didn't have lead shoes—how could they have guessed that it was their rucksack and glasses that were made of lead?"

"So then they thought they had made a mistake,

and attacked two harmless walkers, out for a day in the country."

"And who knows what they've been up to since. Ben—do you suppose Lily and Violet are spies for the Lead-Footers?" The full realization of what had happened began to dawn upon the children.

"Why, we showed them everything!" cried Miranda in horror. "All around the farm——"

"They'll go back and tell the others——"

"We must stop them!" Miranda was immediately ready for action. "I always knew there was something odd about them," she added complacently.

"It's easy to say that, now we know who they are," replied Ben impatiently. "Anyway, we shouldn't be standing here doing nothing. We must think how we can help. It's up to us, because if we leave things as they are until the others get back, it may be too late." Secretly, Ben was delighted at this opportunity of helping the balloonists—how pleased they would be! They might be in terrible danger, because of these two spies—and it was nearly Midsummer Night, too. "How long is it to Midsummer?" he said aloud.

"It's in three nights' time, I think."

"Well, we haven't long—and my goodness, we must go after those two, or they'll slip away altogether."

Neither of the two children had any idea what they would do when they found Violet and Lily, but they set off, nevertheless. After pushing as quietly as possible through bamboo branches, in the direction that the old ladies had taken, they heard faint voices on the other side of the grove. Violet was telling Lily something, and she was replying in meek tones. Then there was the sound of a single pair of footsteps, trudging away.

"That'll be Violet, I expect," whispered Ben, crouching behind a bush. "She said she was going on ahead." They inched nearer and found themselves just behind Lily, who was sitting on the ground, eating a sandwich.

The events of the next few minutes seemed incredible when they thought about them afterwards, but all the same, they did happen. The next thing that Miranda was aware of, was Ben, leaping out from behind his bush and landing squarely on the back of the unsuspecting Lily. "Like someone in a film, it was," Miranda said later. Although Ben was smaller than Lily, he was tall and muscular for his age, and he had the advantage of taking her by surprise—he had not even stopped to tell Miranda what he was going to do.

It's now or never, he thought to himself, and jumped. It was a good thing that he hadn't waited to consider his chances of success, or he might never have done it. To his astonishment, Lily twisted around with tremendous force for an old lady, and with unexpected agility, half threw him off, so that he hit his head on the ground. But at this point, Miranda rushed to help him and sank her teeth into Lily's hand.

Just the way a girl fights, thought Ben, his head clear, even in the midst of the turmoil. However, it distracted Lily, who turned to defend herself against the new attacker, and eventually their combined strength, and the fact that Lily had been taken off her guard, defeated her. She lay panting on the ground, her hands and feet held by the two children.

"Quickly, take off my tie," gasped Ben. Miranda managed to untie it without loosening her hold on one of Lily's feet, and they bound her hands together with the tie. This part wasn't difficult, for all Lily's fighting spirit seemed to have left her, and she made no resistance. During the whole struggle she hadn't uttered a word. Looking at her small eyes, full of malice, Ben wondered how they could ever have been deceived into thinking she was just an innocent old lady.

Ben and Miranda looked at Lily, at a loss as to what to do next, and Lily glared coldly back.

"We must shut her up," said Ben, rubbing his bruised head. "There's a barn near the house which might do."

"She'll get out," objected Miranda. Lily stared back malevolently, as though agreeing with her.

"Never mind, we must risk it."

They marched Lily back to the farm. Strangely enough she no longer walked like a bent old lady, but upright, with firm, young steps, looking twice her previous height.

"Do you know," said Miranda suddenly, as they

reached the barn, "I don't believe she's old at all—it's all makeup." Peering closely into Lily's face, she exclaimed, "Why, I can see the white powder and the lines drawn on top—and I bet that's a wig."

"Of course it is." These words, spat out contemptuously, were the first Lily had spoken.

"Fancy my not noticing, and I'm so interested in disguises!" Miranda was mortified.

"They were in the shade the whole time—that's why we couldn't see them properly," said Ben kindly.

"No wonder they walked all the way to the farm from that hill they showed us! I thought at the time it was a long way for two old ladies."

"Yes, and Violet will be miles away by now," said Lily. She sat down on a bale of straw, her bound hands held in front of her. "You don't mind if I have a tiny rest?" Her voice was mocking.

"I wonder what else we've missed?" said Miranda. "Let's look in her pockets." She made a sudden dive. Thrusting her hand into the pocket of Lily's coat, she drew out a small metal object. Lily gave a curious, frightened squeak.

"It looks like an anchor." Ben turned the piece of metal over in his hand, puzzled. It was light, made of some silver-colored metal, and around it was wrapped a great quantity of fine thread. He started to unwrap some of it, and saw it was fastened to the anchor at one end. "Whatever could it be——?" he began.

"*I* see!" Miranda snatched it away in her excitement. "It's how they get down. Do you remember Leo saying that the balloonists had seen the Lead-Footers go up, but nobody had ever discovered how they got down?"

"I don't see how——" began Ben. "Yes, I do! These were the things that glinted in the air—when we saw the Lead-Footers around the bonfire—before they ascended. If you were in the air——" He spoke slowly, trying to work it out.

"And you threw down the anchor, so that it caught in something, a bush or a clump of grass——" continued Miranda, helping him.

"—then you could pull yourself down to earth, by hauling on the anchor," finished Ben. The children had indeed stumbled on the ingenious way in which the Lead-Footers returned to earth, which until now had been a closely guarded secret. Lily's expression of helpless fury told them that they were right.

A mischievous gleam came into Miranda's eyes. She turned to Ben, who guessed what she was thinking.

"If we—take this away——" Ben threw the anchor on the floor.

"And—remove these——" Miranda whipped away Lily's glasses.

"Then up she goes!" Ben laughed triumphantly. "There's our problem solved."

As soon as Lily lost her glasses, she rose into the air. The barn was a high one, and soon she was floating up to its roof. She couldn't get down because she was

too light, and she had no anchor. She grasped one of the black rafters, and waved her legs helplessly. For a second Ben felt sorry for her, but then he told himself that she was not a dear old lady but a dangerous Lead-Footer, threatening his beloved balloon friends. Furthermore, it was she who had laughed when she thought he and Miranda had been burned in the crashed balloon.

"Nobody will hurt you," he called up to Lily, "but you can stay there until we come for you."

Miranda picked up the anchor and the glasses. "I can't possibly wear these," she said, after trying on the glasses. "I can't hold my head up, they're so heavy."

"Give them to me." Ben put them in his pocket, where they strained the lining to its uttermost.

Miranda searched in her pockets and brought out a packet, a mirror, and one or two tubes. Ben watched, fascinated, as she covered her face with greyish-white color, skillfully drew lines and shadows with one of the lipstick-like tubes, reddened her eyelids, and shook grey powder on her hair, rubbing it well in. "Now, who am I?" she asked, bending slightly, as though she had lumbago.

"An old lady!" said Ben, admiringly.

"I think I've got some cardboard spectacles, too," said Miranda, searching in another pocket. "Yes, here they are." She put them on. "Now I look just like Lily."

A snort of disgust came from the ceiling.

"Well, you don't really look very much like her," said Ben critically, "but you would pass for her in the dark."

"It *is* nearly dark," said Miranda seriously.

"You don't mean—you're not——?"

"Yes, I *am*. I mean to find where Violet is going and anything else I can—there's no time to lose, either."

"She'll be miles away by now, you silly babies," came Lily's soft, mocking voice from the rafters.

"I'm coming too, then," said Ben, ignoring Lily. "I'm not letting you go alone." Ben had made up his mind that if Miranda was going to do anything reckless he was going to be with her. They shut the barn door hurriedly behind them, leaving a silent Lily floating high in the semi-darkness inside. Neither of them stopped to think that it was hardly wise to have let her hear every word of their plan, nor that they hadn't bolted the barn door. They sped off, full of confidence, in the direction of the bamboo grove. Lily pursed her lips and resigned herself to waiting, but not for long.

Chapter 10

PLUMBO'S PLAN

ON THE way to the bamboo grove, where they had last heard Violet, Ben and Miranda skirted around the chicken house where Cornelius was sleeping. Turning a corner, they almost collided with someone walking along through the gathering dusk with purposeful strides. They shrank back immediately, recognizing Violet, but she did not see them.

"I thought she'd gone," Ben whispered. "What a piece of luck." They set off after her, creeping as quietly as possible over the uneven ground. In their excitement at having found her so easily, they had forgotten that the balloonists would soon be coming home, and that they had left not so much as a note to tell their friends why Lily was in the barn; nor did they pause to wonder why Violet had returned to the farm, and had not gone straight to her "head-quarters" as she had arranged.

Once out in the open country it was difficult to stay hidden, but Violet was in a great hurry and never once glanced back. After consulting her watch once or twice, she lengthened her strides. All illusions of old age were gone—she walked as fast as an athletic man, covering the rough, tussocky grass and patches of rock-strewn ground as easily as though they were smooth carpets. Ben and Miranda followed at a distance. They were soon out of breath, in their efforts to keep up with her.

After about half an hour of dodging behind rocks, and then running to keep within sight of their quarry, Ben and Miranda saw Violet cross the road leading from the farm to St. Alfred's. It was now almost dark, and for the first time they remembered the Balloon People.

"They should be coming home by now," said Ben, in a low voice.

"That's why Violet isn't following the road—she's afraid of meeting them," replied Miranda.

She was evidently right, for Violet glanced up and down the road, and then made off on the other side, until she was hidden by some bushes. Following quickly, the children saw her emerge onto another road.

"That's where the road forks," whispered Ben. "We saw it from the balloon. She's safe here."

Sure enough, Violet seemed to relax at this point. She disappeared from view for a moment, and the children drew nearer. There was a loud roar. It was the unmistakable sound of an engine starting.

"Oh, no!" exclaimed Miranda. "After all this!"

With a rush, a long, low, black car shot into the road from its hidden parking place. Ben rubbed his forehead in distress.

"We might have known she would have a car. How stupid of us to imagine she would walk all the way. We may as well give up now." He sat down dejectedly.

The car stopped reversing, its engine roared again, and it swung around. Then its engine stalled. There was silence. Ben jumped up to see Violet get out of the car, slamming the door violently behind her. They could hear her muttering as she lifted the car hood.

Ben and Miranda looked at one another wildly. Ben almost laughed at Miranda's weird appearance in the cardboard spectacles, which she hadn't bothered to take off.

"Now!" he said.

Sometimes there was such a perfect understanding between Ben and his sister that there was no need for explanations. Together, they ran into the road and to the car, its black bulk hiding them from Violet, who in any case was half-hidden by the large hood. They knew that soon Violet would have righted the fault in the engine and they acted quickly as only desperate people can. All was not lost. The handle of the trunk turned at Ben's touch—like every part of that huge and magnificent car, is was well oiled, and moved smoothly and noiselessly. In a flash, they had jumped inside.

It was black as a dungeon inside the trunk, but as the car was so large, it was roomy. There didn't seem to be any other cargo and they were able to hold the lid up slightly so that a faint glimmer of light relieved the gloom. Afterwards, other people who heard the story found it difficult to believe they could have traveled like this, and certainly nobody would say it was a comfortable way of getting from one place to another.

In five minutes they heard a loud slam—the lid of the hood. A jolt was followed by a coughing sound and the car vibrated harmoniously. Violet had cured the engine trouble.

After this the children endured an agony of jerks as they drove at high speed over a bumpy road; the jostling and hard butting of their heads against the trunk as they turned corners; and the bumps, prods and kicks of each other's shoulders, elbows and feet as they strove to hold themselves in position. The car was expensive and smooth-running, but this was not of much help to the children when Violet was driving at breakneck speed, and they were bent almost double.

The journey went on for so long that Ben and Miranda became numbed. In the end they couldn't have told you how long they had been in the car. Then there was an unusual silence. They had stopped.

They waited a short while, but there was no sound. A faint smell of burning drifted through the crack of the trunk lid. Ben lifted it cautiously and a yellow-green light showed them that the car had stopped on grass against what looked like a high wall. As the lid went up, they could hear several voices chattering shrilly somewhere behind the wall. Ben climbed out first, wincing with stiffness. Miranda followed, leaning against the wall for support, as the painful pins and needles in her arms and legs wore off.

In the dim light (for it was a moonless night, and there was only the sickly yellowish flare to see by), dark figures were making their way through what looked like a gap in the wall.

Miranda turned to Ben. "I'm so frightened," she pleaded. "Can't we go away, while there's a chance?"

"If you like," said Ben.

Miranda had lost her nerve for a moment, but she took a deep breath. "No, I'll go in—after all, I can pass for Lily in this dim light, and I think I can act the part."

Poor Miranda, thought Ben, she sounds much less sure of herself than usual. "Look," he said aloud, "here's a chink in the wall." In fact there were many such chinks, as the whole wall was in very bad repair. He put one eye to it and tried another crack. "Yes, I can see something inside and, what's more, I can hear quite well." He put an ear to quite a large hole which he had found. "Go in, and I'll listen and watch as much as I can. If anything goes wrong, I'll fetch help."

Miranda wondered gloomily what might go wrong, and where he would go to fetch help. It was dark, they were in the middle of the countryside, among enemies with fast cars, and they had no business being there. Somehow, though, she felt bound to go on with the plan—whether it was from loyalty to her balloon friends, or just plain stubbornness, she didn't know. So she smiled at Ben, trying to be cheerful.

Ben thought how yellow her teeth looked in the sinister light and felt a chill of fear, but he said, "Must be very wet living in a house with so many holes in the walls." With this attempt at a joke, he watched her go through the stone gateway. Nobody questioned her limping figure. He wondered miserably whether she was acting, or just stiff from the car.

Miranda soon saw the source of the greenish-yellow light. It was a bonfire, like the one they had seen before in the field. Someone standing near it was pouring a substance on the flames—some kind of chemical, she supposed—and they leapt higher, lighting up the small gathering of Lead-Footers, who were sitting on the grass, or standing and talking. There was now no doubt at all that this was one of their meetings, and Miranda felt alone and rather sick. She stood to one side of the group, trying to behave as naturally as possible. She remembered not to stoop, as though she were an old lady, for of course Lily had only been pretending to be old, and would not have stooped when she was among her friends.

"There you are Violet," said a man's voice, making Miranda jump. "Isn't Lily with you?"

"I assume she's coming on later," said Violet. "I thought it advisable that she should arrive separately —safer, you know." She glanced around, and her eyes fell on Miranda, whose legs almost crumpled under her. Now, she thought, I'm done for.

But Violet was not looking at her carefully—she had expected to see Lily, and there she was. At least, she saw a pair of glasses gleaming in the firelight, and a small figure of roughly Lily's height, dark against a darker wall, which was enough to give the impression of Lily. "Glad to see you're here on time," Violet said casually. "Have any trouble?" She didn't even wait for a reply, and Miranda, her heart beating painfully, said nothing. The dangerous moment passed.

How right Pushkin is, thought Miranda. People are so unobservant.

At this point there was a welcome diversion. Everyone was making way for a new arrival, who seemed to be some kind of leader, judging by the respectful way they treated him. Miranda couldn't see properly, as there was a man standing in front of her, but when he moved she saw why—the newcomer was a short, strutting man, not much taller than Ben, and certainly thinner.

He walked with mincing steps to a place near the bonfire, where one of the Lead-Footers placed an orange box for him; he climbed on this, and Miranda had a better view of him. A cigarette hung drooping from one corner of his mouth and a greasy looking lick of hair was slicked across his forehead. He had protuberant eyes and a drooping moustache. He was a most unprepossessing character.

He shifted his heavy feet around on the box for a minute, and then, startling everyone, he went STAMP on the frail wood, cracking it. Miranda gasped with the rest, and immediately they were all attention. The man seemed pleased with this beginning, and he smoothed back his hair with one gloved hand. Having gained his audience, he took out his cigarette, brandished it, and shouted, "We'll bash 'em, that's wot!"

Miranda almost laughed, it seemed so ridiculous— the raptly attentive people, the fierce little man, the stamping and shouting—and yet, she knew that it was all in earnest, and no laughing matter.

Someone in the group called, "That's the stuff, Plumbo!"

"Tell us when!" cried another.

"Let's get at 'em!"

"Tonight!"

One or two of the Lead-Footers began to rock on their feet, and Miranda recognized the beginnings of the dance. A murmuring rose from them—not the pleasant sound of bees or crickets on a summer's day, but a menacing sound, like a distant storm.

Plumbo held up an elegant glove, for silence. "The sky is ours, *ours*." He stamped. "I'm telling yer— they ain't got no right to be there, and we're going to stop 'em, wiv guns, wiv bombs—I'll wipe 'em orf the sky—jest let 'em wait." There was another thud on the box and he paused to draw breath. With his eyes bulging even more, and his face shining with sweat, he was terrifying.

The audience hung on every word, gazing at him rapturously. Even Miranda was half fascinated.

Plumbo continued, his voice rising. "In two nights —jest two nights' time—you orl know wot night it is——"

"Midsummer Night!" cried the people enthusiastically.

"And on that night"—Plumbo lowered his voice dramatically—"you orl knows wot happens. Well, I'll tell yer, so there ain't nobody wot don't know." He paused. "They go up, that's wot! Do they go up fer an hour? No! Do they go up fer two hours?"

"No!" answered the crowd.

"I'll tell yer how long they go up fer." He leaned forward, fixing his bulging eyes upon each one of them in turn. "They go up fer the whole night—*our* time, that's wot it is—they go up in *our* time, and there ain't no room for us and them. It's us *or* them, that's wot I say, and I say we're going to swipe them lot—bash 'em so as they don't never come back."

"On Midsummer Night!" cried Violet, her eyes shining.

"On Midsummer Night!" they all cried together.

The people were becoming frenzied, and a man

115

and a woman near Miranda, who she gathered were called Wylie and Cynthia, began to lift leaden feet in a clumsy dance.

"Give us the word," panted Wylie. He was a giant of a man, and his huge shadow leapt on the stone wall, making him look twice the size.

"We're all waiting for the word," said Cynthia primly. A knife flashed in the green light and Miranda shuddered. Then she saw that it was not a knife, but an anchor. The whole circle pulled out their anchors and waved them, as Ben and Miranda had seen them do before in the field. Miranda pretended to pull one out too, so as not to be noticed.

"Stop!" Plumbo's glove pointed. "First let me tell yer wot the plan is. I've 'eard, from them wot knows, that we're in fer some wind." He gave a thin smile. "And this wind, yer might say, is due around these parts termorrer!"

"You know they have their weathercocks, Plumbo," said Violet, her hands on her hips. "We'd never fool them."

"No," mumbled Wylie, "they won't go out unless the wind's right."

"Wait till yer 'ears the whole story!" Plumbo stamped emphatically. "Yer've only 'eard 'arf of it yet. The cocks will point the way they want ter go— you might arsk how? Well, I'll tell yer. Because we'll fix 'em, yes"—stamp—"fix 'em that way!"

The others waited expectantly.

"Termorrer," said Plumbo softly, "the wind is

blowing hard, out ter sea—see?" He paused. "And, mates, guess who's going wiv it?"

There was another murmur.

"We won't have no fight on Midsummer Night, because they'll be 'arf-way to the North Pole by tea-time termorrer. They won't be wiv us no more, mates. And yer know how they loves the snow!"

They all laughed nastily. Miranda, horrified, realized how simple and yet how effective the scheme would be. The unsuspecting balloonists, getting up early, as they always did on the day after market day, would set off gaily, after consulting their weather-cock friends, on whom they always relied. They would sail inland—as they thought—in the direction the cocks seemed to show, but instead the balloons would be swept out to sea, the most dangerous thing that could happen to a balloon. Probably they would never return. And how would they ever bear the cold of the northern regions, when they had to have huge fires, even at the height of an English summer?

These thoughts were racing round in Miranda's mind, so that she missed the next part of Plumbo's speech. He seemed to have been delegating to various Lead-Footers the jobs of altering the letters on certain weathercocks. East was to become west, and north was to become south, so that none of them would show the true wind direction. The Lead-Footers were now dancing in glee, and could hardly wait to be off on their nasty errand.

"Let me tell yer, mates," Plumbo was shouting at the top of his voice, "I've seen that sky when it was jest ours, before that lot came and barged in—it was the bewtifullest sky wot I ever saw, wiv only us in it. Jest one more day, and that's wot it'll be like again!"

He subsided, perhaps exhausted by so many threats. His speech had done its work, though; their blood was up, and as one person, they waved their anchors. Miranda, in a kind of numbed nightmare, waved hers too. Then Cynthia, standing next to her, took off her shoes.

Miranda looked hastily for an escape route. She had left it too late. Carried away by Plumbo's speech, she had forgotten for a moment how the meeting would certainly end. All the Lead-Footers were undoing their shoes now. She backed into the rough stone wall, wondering frantically where Ben was, and praying that he would save her. Cynthia rose into the air, her stockinged feet held daintily together; another followed, and another. Wylie was almost last, as he was so heavy. This all happened in seconds. The flames flew up, and they all left the ground— except the small, frightened figure of Miranda, who crouched on the grass, hoping nobody would notice her.

The flames burned their brightest. The livid light illuminated every corner brightly, as the feet rose upwards. Miranda stopped breathing for a few seconds, and then let out her breath thankfully. They were gone. She had escaped. At that moment, a small

metal object clinked against the wall and caught in
a tuft of grass. The line grew taut and trembled. With
staring eyes and paralyzed limbs, she saw two enormous hands hauling themselves towards her. The
hands grabbed, digging sharp, hard fingers into her
shoulder, and Violet's face, black with rage, con-
fronted hers.

Chapter *11*

THE COCKS ARE CHANGED

Ben, shocked into leaving his vantage point, ran to the gateway, his first thought to rescue Miranda from Violet. He drew up as he heard a second voice, Wylie's, and then a third, Plumbo's. Creeping cautiously back, he listened and watched again, through the hole in the wall. After all, it might be glorious and heroic to pit his strength against three angry Lead-Footers, but it would not achieve much. Looking through the chink, he could see by the light of the dying fire, that Plumbo and Wylie had indeed descended, by means of their anchors, and were standing around Miranda, their fists waving. She was lying still on the ground—for what reason he couldn't tell.

"I tell you," Violet was saying to Plumbo, "we assumed they were both lost with the crashed balloon —you know, some of the group going to a meeting at Langleymere Lake sent us a report of it." There was a loud stamp and some wild gestures from Plumbo, who seemed to be as furious with Violet as with Miranda.

"*Two* of 'em, you say?" he yelled. "Where's the other one, then, mate?"

At this point, the bonfire went out, as suddenly as it had done on the previous occasion. The next few minutes were a confused muddle of shouting from Plumbo, explanations from Violet and beating on the wall from Wylie, the force of his enormous bulk threatening to knock it down. There was no sound from Miranda.

"Look fer 'em then!" cried Plumbo, in the darkness. "Search him out, if yer know wot's good fer yer."

The commotion spread towards the gateway, and Ben knew that within seconds they would be upon him. It was dark, but they had produced torches by this time—he could see the beams approaching. They would have found him sooner, if they hadn't been so busy arguing with each other, and so lost time.

Plumbo called from inside the building, "I'll stay here wiv this one—I ain't getting no younger, ter be chasing around."

Ben didn't hesitate. He couldn't possibly help Miranda, and there would be no hope at all for any of them if he were caught. He had no chance of escaping, in the dark and in an unknown place. So he opened the trunk of the car, which was still standing where Violet had left it, and quickly, with violently beating heart, climbed in, shutting the lid behind him.

As Ben crouched in the darkness, it was easy for him to judge the whereabouts of Wylie and Violet because of their extreme heavy-footedness. The weather had been so dry that the ground was rock hard and their footsteps vibrated loudly, once disappearing together, then returning, and again covering the ground around the headquarters. Every time they came near the car Ben thought he was lost, but they always blundered away again.

"One can only assume," said Violet's voice, "that the wretched boy has somehow escaped our notice."

"Perhaps he was never 'ere," said Wylie, which for him was quite an intelligent remark, for his brain was rather slow.

"He may be back at the farm—and so might Lily, for that matter," said Violet thoughtfully. "I expect the girl came in a balloon. We ought to go and see if we can find Lily, I suppose—not that she matters much, of course."

Ben felt quite sorry for Lily.

After this there was a long pause. Ben could hear them talking inside the headquarters, but the walls of the car muffled the sound too much for him to be able to distinguish words. For a long time he had to bear the stuffiness of the car, which was like a sealed tin box, and the suspense of not knowing what had happened to Miranda. Eventually, in spite of his fear, he almost fell asleep. This was his second broken night in a row and he was exhausted. He was jolted out of his drowsiness by the car's engine starting. He resigned himself to yet another journey in the trunk. At least, he thought, I couldn't be any worse off, wherever they take me—and it will soon be morning.

Ben's worry about Miranda's safety made the second journey far worse for him than the first. He could hear nothing inside the car, but after a while it stopped, and he heard Plumbo talking to Wylie, so he knew they must have gotten out. He steeled himself against discovery, and made plans to dash away, if they opened the trunk. But other matters were occupying them.

"Get up ter this 'ere cock," Plumbo was saying, "and mind yer fix it like I said."

Then there was a long wait. Eventually, Wylie's clumping footsteps returned.

"I fixed it just right—that is, just wrong, if you see what I mean," he guffawed.

"Get a move on, yer great booby," said Plumbo rudely. The car door slammed and the bumpy journey continued.

This performance was repeated several times. Violet did most of the hard work, rising up to the steeples and roofs by taking off her shoes, and altering the letters on the weathercocks, so that anyone seeing them would think he were flying in a different direction from the true one. The party inside the car became merrier and more and more pleased with their own cleverness. Ben lost count of the number of stops. So weary that he couldn't imagine ever being out in the open air again, he longed to sleep, and yet was much too uncomfortable and worried.

At the next stop, he heard Violet say, "We need to hurry—it's almost dawn."

They seem to be travelling all over the country, altering cocks, thought Ben in despair. We could be anywhere.

Again the car halted, after passing over a particularly bumpy piece of ground. This time, there were sounds of several people getting out, some low discussion, footsteps walking away, and then silence.

I'll count to a hundred, thought Ben, and if they're not back by then, I'll make a dash for it. When he had reached a hundred, he counted another hundred, just to make sure. I'd better go now, he thought, or they'll be back again.

He was right, for when he lifted the lid he heard them in the distance. It was now growing light, and he saw that the car was parked by a stone building of some kind. It looked rather like the Lead-Footers' headquarters. Ben thought, We've been round in a complete circle, but there was no time to ponder, and he didn't really take in his surroundings. He dodged quickly around a corner and waited. Soon he heard the Lead-Footers draw nearer and, to his astonishment, Lily's voice.

". . . I thought you were never coming to rescue little me . . . you can't imagine what a horrid, nasty time I had in that dreadful, hot barn . . . I shouted and shouted for hours, until you heard me at last . . . those beastly children did it, you know . . . shut me up in there . . . I could have been there for days. . . ."

Then Ben looked around him for the first time. The grey light of early morning showed that he was back on the farm! He was so astonished and pleased that he hardly noticed the car drive away. He was safe, and free.

Ben was so overcome with relief that he forgot his tiredness, and stood breathing in great gulps of moorland air. He forgot all his troubles, the changed weathercocks, the fate of Miranda and the need to warn the balloonists in a glorious reveling in his freedom. Then he gradually became aware of something strange. What was it? Something was different from yesterday. As though answering his question, a gust of wind ruffled his hair. As soon as he noticed it, the wind seemed to gather strength. At first it was just a gentle sighing, but soon it was blowing in sturdy gusts, making him rub his arms with cold. Ben thought of the balloonists.

They can't have set off yet. And anyway, Cornelius will warn them that it's going to be a windy day, and that the wind's in the wrong direction. He felt sure that he would find the Balloon People sitting at their bamboo table, and he would be able to explain what had happened the night before, and give them valuable information about the Lead-Footers. He set off eagerly for the house, which was not far away, as the Lead-Footers had brought the car over the grass, almost to the door.

That's odd, he thought, why didn't they hide the car? It seems they weren't afraid of being seen. He had his first foreboding. As he walked, a speck flew in his face—a piece of half-burnt straw. He was picking it off, not thinking much about it, when an un-mistakable smell was borne on the wind from the direction of the house. It was the smell of burning.

Now he broke into a run. He reached the farm-house, which looked much as usual, except that the door was shut. (The balloonists always left their doors wide open, to show how welcome visitors were.) Following the smell, his heart beating fast, and sure by now that something was wrong, he skirted the house and saw an open window. From this was drifting a thin wisp of smoke. He leaned inside and saw on the floor a bundle of smouldering straw. It was the work of minutes to clamber inside and stamp out the sparks. Ben looked up at the roof, the rafters, the dry bamboo furniture, and shivered. It was easy to see what would have happened if the fire had taken hold.

Filled with sudden energy, he ran off to the barns, to see if the Lead-Footers had left any other souvenirs of their visit, for there was no doubt that they had meant to burn down the farmhouse. Perhaps the fire would have spread to the other buildings—they were close enough together.

Ben went first to the barn where they had left Lily. Hours too late, he remembered that they had not locked the door after them. No wonder the Lead-Footers had discovered her so easily. But the door was locked now. He shook the great padlock that secured it, helplessly—nothing short of a file would undo it. He was thinking only that he might find another fire inside the barn, but as he shook the door absentmindedly, there was a scuffling inside. Ben drew back as though the padlock were red-hot. A small voice said: "Please let me out, whoever you are—and I'm *so* hungry."

It was Miranda.

"It's me, Ben," he called through the door. "Are you all right? Is the barn on fire?"

"On fire? What do you mean? Can you get me out? Oh, I knew you would come! Have you got breakfast?"

"Just like you to be always thinking of food," said Ben, but secretly he was delighted that his sister was so much her normal self.

"I heard them say that they would put the key under a large stone out there," called Miranda, pressing herself against the door. "Do hurry!"

Ben turned over one or two stones lying nearby, and in quite a short time—though it didn't seem so to Miranda—he found the key. Miranda emerged from the barn, pale and dirty, but otherwise looking cheerful. Before asking her anything, Ben searched the barn but found no signs of fire.

"They tried to set fire to the farmhouse," he told Miranda. "That's what I had to look for here. How long have you been in the barn, by the way?"

"By the way, indeed," said Miranda, sulkily.

"You know I don't mean it like that!"

"They've just put me in there. They took Lily away, and locked me in instead. Lily was shouting so loudly they soon heard her. At first they were going to put me in the chicken house, but after they found Lily, they shut me in here."

"You must have been in the car all the time then?" Ben was incredulous.

"I suppose they couldn't think what else to do with me. I wasn't hurt or anything, but I think I might have fainted, because I don't remember much of what happened after we left that—horrible place."

"So we were both traveling together," said Ben.

"That's how you came! In the trunk again? I thought perhaps the Balloon People had brought you."

"No sign of them. Still, there are no bones broken, and we must get back to business. We must look in every shed and workshop, Miranda, in case they've left any more fires." She followed him unwillingly, dragging her feet. "Can't we go to the house and get some food?"

Ben was not listening. There was no sign at all of the balloonists. The wind was still rising, and the grey light of early dawn had taken on a pink tinge as the sun rose. "They should be back by this time," he said.

"Where's Cornelius?" asked Miranda, looking up to his usual perch on the farmhouse roof. "He must be still asleep."

"Surely not," said Ben, his heart sinking. By this time his forebodings were certainties. Even Miranda sensed that all was far from well.

They ran together, against the buffeting wind, to the chicken house where Cornelius had retired to sleep the day before. Stooping to pass through the low door, Ben doubled up and coughed as he was enveloped in a thick, sickly smell. Putting his handkerchief to his face, he found a bundle of limp, grey feathers in a chicken's nest. Cornelius lay there, his eyes closed and his head drooping. He made no movement when they touched him.

They laid the cock on the hearth rug and poked up the farmhouse fire, which was so large that it never entirely went out. They had to shut the oak door, as the wind was now whistling around the solid building. Miranda stroked Cornelius's feathers mournfully.

"Do you think he's——?"

"No, of course not," interrupted Ben hastily. "Don't jump to conclusions. I think he's drugged, or gassed." He poured some water down the cock's beak and after a while he moved and croaked hoarsely. He tried to rise and crowed weakly—he hardly seemed to know where he was.

"Lie down, Cornelius," said Miranda, looking at him anxiously. "It's us." Cornelius lifted heavy eyelids and recognized her. He crowed gently.

"Can you tell us what happened?" asked Ben.

"Ate my corn—thought it tasted queer," whispered Cornelius. Ben looked at Miranda as much to to say, Told you so!

"When?" asked Miranda, bending low to catch his faint words.

"Yesterday—old person—couldn't warn Leo. . . ." The cock could say no more.

"Yesterday!" exclaimed Ben. "You know who that'd be? Do you remember—we saw Violet when we had left Lily shut up? She was near the chicken house. I bet it was her that drugged poor Cornelius."

"That'll be why she was delayed so long. She'd have to put Cornelius out of action, or he'd have warned the balloonists this morning."

"It's strange that the Balloon People didn't search for him this morning, though," said Ben. "I wonder why they set off without him?" But Cornelius's eyes had closed again. They would hear no more explanations from him for a while. Miranda looked into his face and saw that he was sleeping peacefully. Now that the cock had recovered, a tremendous wave of tiredness swept over them.

Miranda rose to her feet. "We can leave him here, with the door unlocked—I should think he'll be quite safe."

"I've found some food in the larder," said Ben, who had been looking around. "We'd better eat now and then have a look for fires in the barns."

Outside in the farmyard the scene was desolate. The grey sky was full of fast-racing, ragged clouds, and it was more like a winter's day than a June one. The whole place was quite silent, except for the noise of the rising wind. Not a bird sang, and there was no human voice or smell of good cooking. They were quite alone. Somewhere in that grey sky, their balloonist friends were drifting helplessly.

Ben said what they were both thinking. "There's nothing more we can do here. At least we've put out the fire and looked after Cornelius. I don't think there are any more fires, so we ought to get back to Langleymere."

Miranda noticed that he didn't say, "Go home." "I wonder where they all are now?" She searched the stormy sky. "Do you think they'll ever come back? And what will happen to them if they don't— or if they're blown somewhere very cold—or if they fall in the sea?"

Ben didn't answer. He and Miranda turned and began to walk down the long white road that led to St. Alfred's. They had no idea how they were going to travel the distance to Langleymere. Their clothes were flapping against them in the wind and they felt utterly miserable.

They passed two milestones without speaking. Miranda sat down on the second one, which was a most uncomfortable shape for sitting, but she didn't seem to notice.

"I just can't go any further." Two nights without much sleep, and the strains of all their experiences had put deep circles under her eyes. Ben didn't argue, for he felt the same. He played idly with some windblown buttercups, pulling their heads off, and not knowing what to say.

"Don't pull the heads off the poor buttercups," said Miranda.

Ben threw away the one he was holding and flung himself on the grass. "I don't care if I sleep here all day."

Staring dully into the sky he saw a balloon in the distance. He turned over at once and pressed his face into the cold grass. "I'm so tired, I'm seeing things," he muttered crossly.

But Miranda had seen it too. She stood up, tiredness forgotten, and waved, hardly believing her own eyes. The balloon approached at a tremendous speed and made an inexpert landing some distance away. Ben and Miranda ran eagerly towards it, and saw Felix and Becky already climbing out.

"Well, you see," Felix was saying, "we set off very late this morning, because Leo told us off for not loading up properly. I've never seen him so bad tempered. He said, 'You'll have to catch us up as best as you can, or not come at all'—just like that, and left us to it."

"We finished loading in the end," Becky went on, "but it took us ages. The balance of the basket was all wrong, and there were only the two of us to help. You see, all the children went in the two other balloons—we're not allowed to take passengers, as we've only just been given our balloon-flying certificates."

"So they went on ahead with the others?"

"Yes—half in Mr. Perkins and Pushkin's balloon,

and half in Leo and Emma's. We could see them flying on ahead—going quite fast, they were, as the wind was so strong."

It was not much later in the day, and the four children were flying back to Langleymere in Felix and Becky's balloon. They had waited for hours for the wind to be right.

"I still don't understand why the others didn't notice that the weathercocks were wrong," said Ben.

"Everyone was very upset this morning, because they thought you two had gone off again," replied Felix. "We were hardly talking to each other—you should have seen us. Leo said we should never have trusted you again after the last time—but don't worry, it'll be all right now we know why you went," he added, seeing Miranda's stricken face. "That is— if we ever see them again."

There was a silence.

"It was our fault, letting Violet and Lily go," said Becky, "so you needn't feel that you were to blame. Leo told us to suspect anyone we saw around the farm, and you've done the best you could."

"That wasn't much," said Ben gloomily.

"So we think they must have been too upset to look at the weathercocks properly," Becky continued. "Everything was in a muddle."

"And of course Cornelius was drugged and couldn't warn you," said Ben.

"Yes. There was no sign of him this morning, so

we imagined he must be still asleep. It did seem odd, but nobody liked to disturb him."

"We were *miles* behind the others," said Becky, tears coming into her eyes, "and if only they had set out later——" She sobbed, and couldn't go on.

"The long and the short of it is that they were blown out to sea so quickly," said Felix, "that they couldn't stop themselves in time."

"But you could, through being behind?"

"Yes. We managed to land near the shore, and then took advantage of a brief change in wind direction to get back to the farm. We realized then that something had gone wrong with the weathercocks."

"But why weren't the others blown back, too?" asked Miranda, puzzled.

"They would be—just a short way—but they would be too far out to sea by then for it to make much difference." Felix shrugged his shoulders. "All we can hope for is that they'll land somewhere, but there's no land for hundreds of miles, and it'll be getting colder all the time."

"So there's not much hope?" said Miranda slowly.

"No."

"But what about *this* wind—the one that's blowing us?" asked Ben timidly.

"You mean, why doesn't it blow them back too? Well, for one reason, it's different out at sea—odd things happen there, with the wind—I don't really know much about it," Felix finished abruptly.

There didn't seem anything else to say.

They landed near the tower with scarcely another word spoken. As Felix and Becky took off to return to the farm they called, "We'll pass over tomorrow afternoon, just in case." Felix didn't say in case of what, and that was the last they saw of him, a forlorn figure outlined against the evening sky, bending down to comfort Becky, who was sitting in the bottom of the basket.

Chapter 12

BALLOONWRECK

WHEN Ben and Miranda met Felix and Becky that stormy day, their troubles were over, but the trials of the other Balloon People were only just beginning. Pushkin and Mr. Perkins were sailing ahead, and a disgruntled pair they were, too. They swept up into the sky, gaining height at a tremendous rate.

"I would never have thought those two would dec-c-ceive us," hissed Pushkin, glancing at the nearest weathercock in the most careless manner as they passed over the first village, Ravenscombe. "And even Cornelius-s is as-sleep, when he should be on duty." He gave a bad tempered growl and recklessly emptied twice the number of sandbags he needed. The balloon careered upwards, swaying and whirling.

"I know you think it was your fault," said Mr. Perkins, with his hands over his eyes as usual, "but actually we were all mistaken about those two children, yes indeed."

"Oh yes, we were!" cried a small child, bouncing up.

"Sit down, sit down," said Mr. Perkins irritably. "And be calm and collected like me." He shook with fright as the balloon's course became more erratic. Pushkin didn't seem to care what he did with the balloon this morning, but he supposed the mood would wear off.

Pushkin pulled his yachting cap further over his eyes and scowled straight ahead; little did they know that he was paying no attention to the navigation of the balloon. They were speeding along, so high that the ground was almost hidden by low clouds.

The balloon's navigator was thoroughly upset, and its passengers weren't looking out, so it was not surprising that nobody noticed the ground below. It was gradually becoming browner and yellower. Light green fields and dark green woods were giving way to sandy patches and yellowish fields, then to yellow shrubs and brown, salt-dried grass, and then to sandy beaches. No one in the balloon noticed these interesting changes. So it was that at 11 a.m. precisely, when Mr. Perkins rose to make their elevenses, and stretched his arms above his head and yawned, and emptied some old carrot leaves—which someone had carelessly left in the pot—over the side of the basket, he gave an undignified squeak, turned as white as his starched collar, and would have fallen out if one of the children hadn't pulled him back by his furled umbrella.

Mr. Perkins had found himself looking down at the great, rolling waves of the Atlantic Ocean, flecked with foam by the rising wind. He sank back, almost fainting.

"Say it isn't true," he moaned. "My dear Pushkin, say it isn't true!"

He spoke so urgently that he aroused Pushkin from his sulks, and the cat glanced languidly over the side. He sprang up, hissing in alarm, and jumped around the balloon basket, consulting every instrument in a frenzy. He whipped out the maps, their folds flapping in the wind, and consulted them upside down in his agitation. Meanwhile, Mr. Perkins revived slightly, as the children gave him sips of heather wine.

Pushkin had never been so much at a loss in his life. He knew how dangerous it was to sail out to sea—there were thousands of miles between themselves and America, and only a few scattered islands on which to land. And it would become very cold as they drew further away from land. They had no warm clothes with them, either. Pushkin sat down on a basket in despair, his head in his paws.

"I'm sure the weathercock at Ravenscombe pointed south," he cried, "and we must have sailed north to be where we are. I made a terrible mistake! Whatever shall we do?"

Mr. Perkins thought. Pushkin had never before made a mistake, so why should he now? His eyesight was the best at the farm—everyone looked up to him as the best balloonist they had. "Then something's afoot, Push," he said, "but never mind, never mind. Got to get back somehow." As he spoke, he proudly lifted up his head and the ropes creaked and strained

as the wind hit them. Ugly black clouds were building
up ahead of them. Mr. Perkins clapped his hat firmly
on his head in a determined way, but he didn't feel
as confident as he looked—he knew they were sailing
straight into a storm. The children stared from Pushkin to Mr. Perkins with round, startled eyes. They
didn't know the danger they were in, but they sensed
something was wrong.

Pushkin was pulling himself together by this time.
He had to make some effort to save them, even if it
were hopeless from the start. He scanned the sky with
his telescope, searching in vain for Leo and Emma's

balloon. He found nothing. The air currents at sea were different from the land ones—they twisted and spiraled like whirlpools. Leo and Emma must be miles away. None of them had ever sailed over a big ocean in stormy weather before, and Pushkin knew that anything could happen.

"Now," said Mr. Perkins briskly to the children, "it's *Them*—causing us a spot of bother, you know. Let me see you all lie down and have a little nap." (Of course, Mr. Perkins had no idea that he had hit upon the truth when he said that their troubles were due to Them.)

There was a murmur of protest from one or two of the children. Sleep—at lunch time! But when they heard that *They* were involved, they did as they were told, grumbling a little to each other. The rocking of the balloon soon made them drowsy and some of them even fell into a fitful sleep.

The gusts of wind had by this time grown into a fresh breeze, and then into a mischievous squall, hurling the balloon about the sky. Soon it would be a gale, and above them the mass of dark clouds was going to engulf their frail little balloon at any moment. It wasn't yet raining, but the wind was the worst that Mr. Perkins and Pushkin had ever faced. Still, they meant to fight with every muscle they possessed. They faced grimly towards the black clouds, and waited for the storm.

Almost at once it was upon them. They were enveloped in dark, damp clouds which swirled thickly around their faces. One or two of the children whimpered as they felt the cold.

"Cover yourselves up in the blankets," ordered Mr. Perkins. Luckily they had brought a few blankets, thinking that they would have a picnic on the grass at lunchtime.

The balloon spun like a top as the wind hit it with full force.

"Splice the main-rope!" yelled Pushkin above the whistling wind. Mr. Perkins looked where he was pointing and saw that one of the ropes was almost frayed in two, under the tremendous strain of the gale. He knew that if the rope broke the basket would be thrown out of balance, and might go completely out of control. So Mr. Perkins seized the two ends of the rope, and with almost superhuman strength, held them together with one hand and bound them. He then tied his bowler hat on more firmly with string, as the wind was threatening to blow it off. Pushkin had a new respect for Mr. Perkins after this—he was magnificent, quick off the mark and full of resourcefulness.

All this time, as Pushkin and Mr. Perkins struggled to keep the basket on an even keel, it was almost dark inside the basket, and the cloud was chilling them all to the bone. They knew that below were only the icy, lashing waves. They also knew that balloon baskets do not float.

The wind began to howl like a hundred demons let loose, and then there was a new sound, which was

As Mr. Perkins stood there, his head fuddled, and not quite sure whether he were drowned or not, Pushkin was picking his way over the beach, screwing up his nose in disgust.

"How can a cat," he complained, "be expected to walk on these boulders?" He examined a broken claw and miaouwed crossly. "Perkins, do you s-see where we are?"

"No, where?" Mr. Perkins's mouth fell open foolishly.

"On a beach, of cour-rse. How unobser-rr-vant you are!"

"I thought we might be." Mr. Perkins's brain might have had sea water in it, for it was working very slowly.

Pushkin continued patiently: "If we'd landed a few minutes earlier, we'd have been in the sea. As it is, we're on an island."

"Oh," said Mr. Perkins.

At this moment there was a mewing sound, like a basket of kittens might make. It came from the balloon. Mr. Perkins and Pushkin stumbled over the pebbles to the basket, and saw that it was not much damaged after all. The basketwork had splintered in the rough landing on the beach, and it was half overturned. Mr. Perkins must have been thrown out when they landed; Pushkin had been entangled in the ropes. The inside of the basket was a mass of tumbled blankets and other equipment. The mewing came from underneath.

A tousled head poked out. It was one of the children.

"I've been asleep," he said, rather unnecessarily.

"Want my tea," piped another voice from underneath the heap.

The heap heaved and the children climbed out, looking around without surprise.

"What shall we have for tea?" said Pushkin.

"And here's the map." It was a few hours later, and Mr. Perkins and Pushkin were sorting out the contents of the balloon basket. Mr. Perkins held up the map, which was blotched with sea water but still readable. "Show me where you think we are, Pushkin."

"Ha!" snorted Pushkin. "I *know*. We're here!" A striped paw blotted out a small island a few miles off the coast from which they had come.

"I don't know, don't know, Push," muttered Mr. Perkins doubtfully, "whether we could paddle back . . . in the inflatable raft, you know . . . has been done, I daresay . . . very doubtful whether . . . in the circumstances . . . not certain that . . ."

"We'll be ther-r-r-re by morning," purred Pushkin persuasively. He rummaged in a nearby pile and pulled out a bright green object. He began to take deep breaths and blow into a valve, his eyes bulging in the most alarming way. "Just——" (puff), "blow it up——" (gasp). "Nothing to it, you see. . . ." He let out all his breath in a rush. "Wish I had my

146

bicycle pump. The thing is, Perkins, we must be back by tomorrow, and well you know it."

"I do agree, Pushkin. I realize the seriousness of our position as well as you do, I hope." Mr. Perkins raised his chin proudly above his collar, once so starched and glorious, now sodden and sadly yellowed by sea water.

While Mr. Perkins was making this last remark, Pushkin had blown up the raft, attached a sail, packed an emergency provisions box, laid out enough lifebelts for Mr. Perkins, himself and the balloon children, set out blankets in the bottom of the raft and written a note on the empty shell of a gull's egg, which he then hid inside a cairn made of pebbles. "To tell others we've been here," he said, by way of explanation for the last action. At the same time he casually balanced a pebble on one paw, twirling it like a juggler.

"My dear-r-r Perkins," he drawled, "there's nothing her-re but pebbles and seagulls—I r-really can't wait to get away from such a very boring place."

An admiring audience of balloon children and sea birds were sitting on the pebbles in rows, watching all this. The children were thrilled to be taking part in such an exciting adventure. They had been provided with an excellent tea of seaweed and pineapple patties, and had complete faith in Mr. Perkins and Pushkin to get them home again.

"We'll show those Lead-Footers," said Mr. Perkins, cheering up considerably.

"We'll show them!" echoed the children.

"They cer-rr-tainly don't expect us back yet," miaouwed Pushkin. "If at all," he added under his breath. "Hop in!"

The children eagerly hopped. The raft sagged a little, but it held, and they helped Mr. Perkins on board, as it was pushed into deeper water. Pushkin waded out with it, carrying a paddle that he had improvised from two ping-pong paddles and a broomstick. (Though what any of these articles had been doing in the balloon in the first place, it was hard to say.)

Mr. Perkins sat rigidly at one end of the raft as they left that shore forever, a solemn, black-suited figure. Pushkin leaned on his paddle, and sang a mocking little song to the rising moon.

"And *what* night is it tonight, children?" Pushkin was saying.

"Midsummer Night!" they chorused.

"And *where* do we go then?"

"Up in the air!"

"For *how* long?"

"All night long!"

Pushkin was paddling the last weary lap of their journey—a lighthouse was in sight, which he knew was only a mile or two from the farm. His fur was matted with white particles of sea salt and irritating bits of grit were stuck between his toes, but on his whiskered face was a triumphant grin.

148

Chapter 13

SEA BREEZES

IN THE vast expanse of sky over the Atlantic Ocean, another balloon, victim of the Lead-Footers, was drifting helplessly. Like Pushkin, Leo had consulted a false weathercock as they flew past that morning, and had been blown out to sea before he realized the danger. Luckily, the mass of black cloud that had caused the downfall of the other balloon had missed them, but it was now evening, and they had made no headway in returning to land. They were not traveling fast, nothing spectacular was happening to them, but they were simply drifting along at a maddeningly slow speed and getting nowhere.

"I do believe," said Leo, looking over the side of the basket and consulting the map, "that we've passed over that island before. I remember those large creatures on it—seals, they must be. We must be sailing in a circle." The "seals" were Pushkin and Mr. Perkins, too busy with the raft to look up.

Emma wrung her hands. "Oh dear, oh dear! We could go around in circles forever! Poor Pushkin—poor Mr. Perkins—poor, poor children!" At the thought of the children, tears poured down her cheeks.

The children who were passengers in this balloon looked as if they, too, would cry at any moment.

"Now, now," said Leo soothingly, "it's not so bad. Don't be down in the dumps. We're drifting very slowly and we've missed the storm, by a good piece of luck. All we have to do is wait until morning, when the wind will blow us in to land, without any trouble at all."

"How can you be sure of that?" sobbed Emma.

"Because," said Leo patiently, "every morning, usually, the wind blows *towards* the land. It's for a scientific reason you wouldn't understand," he added grandly. "What really worries me," he went on, "is how we came to be out here in the first place. Shouldn't be at all surprised if They haven't got something to do with it—it'd be just like Them to tamper with those weathercocks. Full of mean little tricks they are. I shouldn't have left this morning, until I'd sorted out what happened to Ben and Miranda, I knew it."

"They haven't gone over to Their side, then?" piped a small child's voice.

"No, they have *not!*" said Leo, quite fiercely for him. "I must admit, I did have my doubts at one time, but a finer pair of kids I never saw in all my balloon days."

The balloon children looked impressed at this praise. Emma, who had complete confidence in Leo, said, "Well, if all we've got to do is wait until morning, we'd better all keep warm." She began spooning out peppermint-orange water ices into plastic bowls. "But what about the other poor children——?" She was on the point of crying again.

"They're safe, I'm sure," broke in Leo hastily. "Now don't you worry, you'll frighten the children. You know perfectly well that Pushkin is the best balloonist you, me, or anyone else has seen—he'll look after them."

Emma, comforted, turned to the task of warming up her children with large helpings of ice cream.

The short summer's night had come to an end, and the children were sleeping peacefully.

"We're losing height," said Leo.

"But there's the shore!" cried Emma excitedly.

"We need to go a little faster if we don't want to land in the sea." Leo searched the basket for ideas.

"*I* know!" Emma pulled out the bamboo pole used for hanging out washing, the same one that Ben and Miranda had admired on their first journey.

"Yes!" cried Leo, grasping her idea at once. "Where's the washing?"

"There's always washing where there's children," said Emma cheerfully, and produced a huge bundle. Quickly they fixed it to the pole and hung it from the side of the basket. At once the wind filled the sheets, towels and small shirts, like so many sails, and the balloon moved faster. Emma laughed happily, and took off her apron, adding it for good measure to the collection. She and Leo held hands as they floated gently low over the sea, giggling together as though they had been out on a joy-ride, and not one which could have ended in disaster.

The children awoke to find themselves on a familiar shore.

"And *what* night is it tonight, children?" asked Emma.

"Midsummer Night!" they cried together, little knowing that a short distance down the coast, hidden only by a headland, their brothers and sisters were saying the same words.

Chapter 14

FOOTPRINTS ON A WALL

"Isn't it odd," said Miranda, spreading marmalade on her last piece of toast, "that Mummy didn't notice we weren't here last night?"

"Nor the night before, come to that—but then, people are so very unobser-rr-vant, as Pushkin would say." Ben imitated Pushkin's drawl well and Miranda laughed. Then they both fell silent and an atmosphere of gloom settled over the room.

"Wherevy'been?" asked Daniel, round-eyed.

"You wouldn't understand, Dan, even if I told you." Ben gloomily stared out of the window. "It seems impossible now, doesn't it, Miranda? I sometimes wonder if it all really happened."

"Well, we only came back yesterday," said Miranda. "What will Felix and Becky do, now they're on their own? I do wish we could help somehow."

"I'm sure the others will get back to the farm."

"But how? Oh Ben, I'm so worried about them. And what's more, do you know what tonight is?"

"Midsummer Night. I have a feeling that tonight is terribly important for the Balloon People—that it will decide things somehow—between them and the Lead-Footers, I mean. I can't explain."

"I know what you mean. But how can they fight, if they're not even here to do it? And Felix and Becky can't take on all the Lead-Footers single-handed."

"Anyway," said Ben, "would you take on even one Lead-Footer?"

"No," admitted Miranda, shivering. "I was so frightened that night in their headquarters. And supposing there are some in this very village—do you think there could be?"

"I'm ready to believe anything now," said Ben. "Sometimes it's just a question of looking properly."

Daniel was listening to their talk with great interest, not understanding much, of course. He wriggled to get down from his chair.

At this point their mother came in and said, "Have you finished, then? I'm taking Daniel out shopping now, so you two can do what you like."

"Want to go 'Anda an' Ben!" protested Daniel, sure he was missing something.

"We're not doing anything exciting," Miranda reassured him. Our adventures really are over now, she thought.

"Come on," said Ben unenthusiastically. "We'll go for a walk."

Their feet carried them automatically to the tower, though they had no reason for going there until the afternoon, when Felix and Becky said they would pass over.

"Oh Ben, I'm so worried about them all," said

Miranda for the tenth time. "Do you think they're drowned?" Tears came into her eyes.

"Of course not," said Ben.

"No one here, as usual," said Miranda, flinging herself on the grass. "It surprises me that none of the children from the village have ever found this place."

"Oh, I suppose they know about it," said Ben, not interested. "They just don't bother to come this far."

"There are one or two footprints, though—someone's been here," said Miranda, looking at the ground. "Quite heavy, too."

"Yes," said Ben, who was scratching his name into the soft stone facing that covered part of the stone walls. "They would be deep—after the rain last night." He idly scratched further up.

Miranda traced the outline of the print with her finger and then examined the next one. "Strange," she said. "There aren't any patterns on the footprints, like you usually get—they're just very deep outlines." Having nothing better to do, she stood in two of them, a foot in each, and began to follow them with her feet. She reached the wall. "My goodness!" she exclaimed, so sharply that Ben turned around.

"You're getting in my way," he complained. "I'm writing here." Then he followed her eyes to the last footprint. The footsteps *continued up the wall*.

Without a word, Ben disappeared through the gateway. In a moment he returned to where Miranda was still gazing, stupefied, at the footprints. "I found them," he said.

"Found what?" Miranda was still absorbed by the footprints. "Ben, how could anyone walk up a wall?"

"If you look carefully," said Ben, "you'll see they're going down, not up. And come outside a minute." He pointed to where the ground had been churned up, just outside the gateway. "What," he said grimly, "made those, do you think?"

"A car?"

"Right." Ben seized Miranda's shoulders in excitement. "*Now* do you see? Who walks down walls?"

Miranda's mouth fell open. "Not——?"

"Yes!" Ben danced madly round her. "We were *here*, last night—it's quite funny, when you think of it! They brought us here—to this tower. Miranda, these are the headquarters of the Lead-Footers! We didn't notice, what with the darkness and watching them, that it was *our* tower. Those are the marks the car made, and those footprints inside, down the wall— that's where Plumbo or somebody walked down when he caught you—like mountaineering on a cliff face, you see!" Ben was beside himself with excitement.

"It looked so different last night," said Miranda slowly. "But these prints are very deep——"

"Of course they are! That's why they have no pattern—they're the prints of lead shoes, Miranda. This is the place all right. It's all been going on under our very noses, in our own village. We've never seen the Lead-Footers before because we've never been here at night, and I suppose everyone else in the village has always been asleep, or watching television."

"And no one would see their bonfires, because of the trees in between, except from the air—then they would think it was leaves being burnt, or something."

The two children stared at each other. "We must tell Felix and Becky, of course," said Ben. "I wonder if they know where the Lead-Footers' headquarters is?"

"Lot of use it will be, them knowing." Miranda was gloomy again.

"We'll tell them, all the same. Would you believe it—we were here all the time. . . ." Ben looked at the footprints again and again. He couldn't get over his discovery.

"So you see," Miranda was rapidly recounting to Felix and Becky, "these are their headquarters!"

"When I can get a word in edgeways," laughed Felix, "*we* have something to tell you! And it's even more interesting."

Becky broke in happily. "They're back—all of them—at the farm! Isn't it marvelous?"

"You mean—Pushkin, and Emma, and——?" Miranda and Ben were astonished.

"Yes, all of them—quite safe. They've lost one of the balloons, but they're busy making another already."

"Oh, Becky," said Miranda guiltily, "and we didn't even ask if you'd heard anything."

"Well, Pushkin and Mr. Perkins crashed on an island——" began Becky.

"No time to explain all that now," interrupted Felix. "The point is, that now they're back—which we came to tell you, by the way—and now we've found out where the Lead-Footer's headquarters is, things are entirely different. There's not much time, of course, before tonight, but we might possibly take them by surprise." He paused thoughtfully.

"Do the others know we weren't to blame, for their being blown out to sea, I mean?" asked Ben.

"Yes, yes, don't worry about that," said Felix. "They guessed it was Lead-Footers' work, after a bit."

"Do you think they might fight the Lead-Footers tonight, then?" asked Ben, brightening up at the prospect of a battle.

"But isn't it dangerous—won't someone be hurt?" asked Miranda, looking anxiously from one face to another.

"Look, Miranda," said Becky, "it's now or never. If we don't fight now, we'll never be free in the sky again."

Felix was already planning the campaign. "First," he said, "Becky and I will return to the farm and let the others know your news—that'll soon cheer them up. You and Ben must stay here. This is what we'll do. . . ." His voice dropped, and he unfolded a plan, perfect in its daring and in its simplicity. "They'll be here before dark, don't forget, wanting to light their bonfire," he ended, "and they should be sure of themselves, and off their guard, thinking we're at the North Pole."

"But what about the balloon children?" Miranda was still worried.

"They'll be safe, don't worry." Felix looked up at the sky. "Going to rain, as I thought," he said. "We often get heavy storms in June. We have to change the weathercocks back, on the way home, so we'd better be off."

In five more minutes their balloon was a distant globe in the sky.

There was a heavy crack of thunder and a few large drops of rain fell on the tower. Farmers all over the country looked at the sky and said, "Time we hurried with that hay." People arranging cricket and tennis matches looked up and shook their heads: "Not much chance of a dry pitch/court tomorrow." Ducks looked up and wagged their tails at the thought of a good day's fun in full ponds. Holidaymakers looked up and sighed at the prospect of a washout. Far away, Cornelius turned up his coat collar and growled, "I feel a storm in my bones!"

Chapter 15

MIDSUMMER NIGHT'S BATTLE

AND so began, in that long Midsummer twilight, the famous battle—for so it was to become—between the Lead-Footers and the Balloon People, for the possession of the sky. It started quietly enough. At dusk, the tower was deserted. The sky was overcast, but the rain had not yet begun, though it threatened to at any moment. There was the sound of a car engine in the distance, and as it drew nearer and stopped near the tower, loud voices floated through its open windows. The doors were flung open and out spilled the Lead-Footers, laughing, talking, mocking the Balloon People, and churning up the fresh green grass with their lead shoes, like tanks.

Birds flew up into the trees in alarm at this disturbance.

"Got yer anchors and lines, mates?" shouted Plumbo, picking up a stone and hurling it into the nearest tree. "Ha! Nearly copped that bird, I did!" A frightened bird flew away, escaping from this ugly, noisy human.

"We ain't 'arf going to 'ave a good time tonight, ain't we, Plumbo?" said Wylie, tramping into the tower through the gateway.

"You bet," said Violet. "Now we've disposed of those wretched people, we'll never have to worry about them again."

"Isn't there really not the teeniest weeniest little chance of their coming back?" piped Lily.

"I do hope not," said Cynthia in alarm, stopping in her tracks.

"Not on yer life," boasted Plumbo. "Them lot is where nobody can help them, that's wot." He gave a coarse laugh. There was a rustle in the bushes and he turned sharply. "Wish I could get rid of every bird and animal wot's in this wood," he said angrily. "Liketer have it ter meself, I would."

The ill-assorted band went through the gateway in single file, as it was so narrow, and once inside laid out their fire. There was a distant rumble.

"It's going to rain, Plumbo," said Wylie.

"Come orf it!" was Plumbo's reply. "Get a move on wiv laying them sticks."

As if mocking him, a large blob of rain fell on his head. Several more ran down his face.

"I don't see why we should attempt to ascend in the rain," said Violet firmly. Like someone turning on a tap it began to pour down; it was the kind of rainstorm, short but heavy, that often comes in the middle of summer.

"Ooooh—I shall get my poor little feet wet!" squeaked Lily. "I don't know what you people are doing, but I'm off to the car to keep my tootsies dry."

"Me, too," said Cynthia at once, "it's mad to get wet for nothing."

She and Lily clumped off, followed by the others, Plumbo grumbling to himself. They shut the car windows and sat quarreling inside, like wasps buzzing in a bottle. Soon rain was falling in torrents, washing around the tower in swirls, carrying earth and stones down the hill, and turning the ground into a mass of sticky, slippery mud.

The tower looked almost like a lighthouse in a stormy sea, the rain was so dense, and the view from the car windows was blotted out by sheets of grey rain driving down them. Something else was happening, too. The ditch around the tower was filling up. Only the heaviest rainstorm would have done it, but gradually it was becoming a swirling, brown moat, full of leaves, moss and sticks. Now the tower looked more than ever like a castle. Insects and animals living in the ditch scuttled to safety—they were astonished to see their home so unusually wet. Another rustle came from one of the bushes where Plumbo had been standing.

The group inside the car were spitefully digging their elbows into each other by this time. Lily pulled Violet's hair, she gave Lily a sly kick in return. Violet pinched Cynthia, who squealed.

" 'Ow much longer is this 'ere rain going on?" said Wylie.

Plumbo peered through the steamy windows and opened the door a crack. "It's O.K., mates, yer can come out and get on wiv the meeting."

The rain had stopped as suddenly as it had begun, but the Lead-Footers scuttled into the tower, not looking to right or left, as though they expected it to start again. By now it was almost dark. Trying to make up for lost time, and very cross indeed, they hurried Wylie on, as he began to make the fire.

"Fine waste of time, that wretched rain," said Violet, her hands on her hips. "Another stick on the left hand side, Wylie."

Wylie looked up sullenly, "Do it yerself, if you can do it better," he muttered.

"Well," said Lily brightly, "here we are, everyone. What a delightful time we're going to have! Let's see a smile or two!"

They looked even more bad tempered.

"Jest think," said Plumbo, "jest think, mates, wot it'll be like up there, wiv only us. It's a bit later than wot we thought, but we'll make up fer that, won't we, mates?"

They all cheered up and Violet and Lily began to dance. The darkness was now complete, as the moon had not yet risen.

"Git a move on and light that bonfire!" said Plumbo to Wylie. Wylie fumbled in his pocket for the matches. His clumsy hands found them, then dropped them on the grass. He peered shortsightedly for them, and in the end trod on them, the matchbox splintering. The others were shifting impatiently from one foot to the other.

" '*Ere* we are," said Wylie at last. "Carn't see a thing——"

"Coooeee!" called a sweet voice. "Can't you light your fire? What a shame!"

The Lead-Footers swung around all together. "Wot's that?" said Plumbo sharply.

"*Who*'s that, you mean," corrected Violet, looking round with narrowed eyes.

The mocking voice came again. "Here I am! Can't you see-ee me? Come and get me!"

The Lead-Footers scattered around the circular grass plot, bumping into each other in the dark.

"I'll bash yer," shouted Plumbo, enraged. "Show yerself, why don't yer?" He held up his fist and shook it, but since it was dark, nobody could have seen it.

"But I'm *here*," insisted the sweet voice, "right in front of you!"

Wylie charged at the wall blindly, like a bull. He grazed his head and bellowed angrily.

"I know all about you," continued the voice, now in a different place. "Shall I tell everyone who you are?"

"I know who it is," said Violet, who had been listening more carefully than the others, "it's that wretched girl again."

"But—she was shut up in the horrid barn," said Lily, bewildered.

"Well, she must have got out of the horrid barn," answered Violet grimly. "It's her all right. Come and help me deal with her."

"I'm waiting!" called Miranda (for it *was* she) from the gateway.

The Lead-Footers dashed towards her voice, passing in single file through the narrow gate, with never a glance at where they were treading. Miranda skipped around the tower, her voice coming from one place and then another. "Wheee! It's a lovely night for ducks!" she mocked.

The Lead-Footers, Violet leading, turned sharp right outside the gate, determined on revenge. "This time you won't——" The rest of Violet's threat was lost as she fell up to her neck in brown, thick, cold water. This was so unexpected that the others, like sheep, couldn't stop themselves, and they all slithered down the muddy side of the ditch, piling on top of one another and striking out blindly at each other in the water. There was complete confusion. Muffled shouts, gurgles and watery coughs came from the struggling mass in the ditch. For some time they floundered helplessly, as the darkness made it difficult to find the bank and their arms and legs were tangled. Wylie lost his head and started hitting out wildly at anything that came his way, thinking it was Miranda. Eventually he found the bank and heaved himself out, like some muddy monster, and lay panting there.

The scheme had been successful beyond Miranda's wildest hopes. She couldn't suppress a giggle. By this time Plumbo had emerged from the ditch, his hair and moustache plastered down by weeds and his soaked gloves clinging to his fingers—his cigarette had disappeared into the water. "I 'eard yer," he yelled, beside himself with rage. "Yer've got it coming ter yer now—yer jest wait." He swiveled around, looking for Miranda and paying no attention to the others, who were trying to climb up the treacherously muddy banks. Cynthia was already sitting on the edge, no more fight in her.

A faint glow lit up the tower—it was the rising moon. At the same time, as Plumbo was rushing in various directions, not sure where to attack, a meow came from above their heads.

"Rr-r-really, what a ver-r-ry foolish fellow!"

Plumbo and Wylie looked up. There was the dark shape of a balloon basket, swinging low over the tower, and lit up by the moon a grinning cat's face leaning over the side. Forgetting Miranda immediately, Plumbo ran into the tower as fast as his lead shoes would allow. "Now yer've been really stoopid," he shouted. "We'll bash yer, knock yer fer six." He began to take off his shoes and so did Wylie, close behind him. Violet and Lily followed, dripping with water. Cynthia was lagging behind. At the gate she turned suddenly and ran away into the trees. Nobody stopped her. The Lead-Footers were so wet that they rose into the air unevenly, weighed down by their waterlogged clothes. As they rose, Pushkin poured out some sand and floated higher.

The sand sprayed on Plumbo's wet hair and moustache, sticking to them. With a shout of rage, he made a dive for the balloon, but it swung away from him.

"It's only a cat," cried Wylie. "We'll settle him!" The Lead-Footers were now all in the air.

"Only a cat?" muttered Pushkin. "We'll see about that!" He sprang on to the edge of the basket and glared directly into Violet's face. He hissed, his eyes like red coals; he swelled himself up to twice his size and fluffed out his tail; every hair stood on end and every claw was unsheathed. He growled savagely. Violet drew back.

"It's a demon cat!" cried Wylie, terrified.

Pushkin spat and made as if to spring on Wylie's

167

head. Wylie swayed away hastily. The Lead-Footers hardly dared even look at Pushkin, he was so terrifying. They held off, not knowing what to do.

Pushkin then gave an ear-piercing shriek, arching his back. Immediately, as though it were a signal—which of course it was—a child's piping voice floated up from below: "Is this the place?"

"Yes," answered another, "Miranda said it was." Then there was a chattering like starlings of children's voices.

Plumbo looked down sharply. "Wot, more of them?"

"It's only some children," called Violet contemptuously. "We must get rid of this cat——" She stopped. Pushkin had gone. He had thrown out some more sand, risen quickly, and was now a hundred yards away.

"Lower yer anchors," said Plumbo, trying to be decisive. "They're only a lot of kids—soon finish them orf and then yer can dry yerselves out. Git moving."

'I wonder why those children aren't in bed at this time?' Violet thought doubtfully, but after hesitating a moment she followed Plumbo.

The Lead-Footers threw down their anchors so that they could return to earth. Some of the anchors were caught in grass, others on stones. The anchors' lines showed up quite clearly in the moonlight. They began to climb down their lines, infuriated by the childish chatter below.

"Wait till I get my 'ands on them kids," muttered Wylie.

They had scarcely begun to descend before they were aware that the circle of grass inside the tower was suddenly filled with people. They seemed to have sprung from nowhere, but they were definitely not children, they were all looking up as though they meant business and, most frightening of all, they held in their hands shiny, steel scissors!

Leo bounded up and down gleefully. Those children did their job really well, he thought. The balloon children, hidden in the bushes, sat down, their part over.

Before the Lead-Footers had time to realize their danger, the balloonists, assembled down below and brandishing their scissors like swords, bounded into action. The cold moonlight flashed on colder steel, which made graceful circles in the air. Snip! The first line was cut—with a howl, Wylie floated upwards, deprived of his lifeline. Snap! Another razor-sharp edge cut Plumbo's line—he flew up, blown here and there by the wind, yelling the whole time. One by one they were all cut loose. The balloonists didn't pause to gloat, but ascended quickly in balloons that they had hidden nearby, and set off in pursuit of the Lead-Footers.

It wasn't long before the balloonists caught up with their enemies, who by this time were so scared that they hadn't the wits to keep upright in the sky, but were wildly out of control. Plumbo was floating upside down and waving his arms and legs furiously.

Leo, sailing one balloon, leaned out. He had no wish to punish the Lead-Footers further. "Do you agree to share the sky with us?" he called to Plumbo.

"Not on yer life!" yelled Plumbo, trying to tilt the balloon's basket as it flew past. Emma shot at him with a water pistol. His threats were promptly drowned.

Ben, in the other balloon, fired another pistol which he had found in the basket, as Wylie seized the side of it. It was not a water pistol but an ink gun—Wylie turned Prussian blue and fell away. Ben watched him fall, fascinated.

"*Now* do you surrender?" shouted Mr. Perkins sternly, pointing his umbrella at Plumbo. "We shall leave you alone, but you must promise never to come near us again."

Leo aimed another pistol at Violet, who was within shooting distance. "Say yes, say yes!" she cried desperately to Plumbo.

"Say you will!" shouted Lily, speeding past him.

Plumbo had had enough. "Let me down, will yer?" he shouted. "Come on, mate, let me down!"

"Hm," said Leo, "not what I would call a surrender. However, it's probably the best we'll get. Haul them in!"

Ben privately thought that the Lead-Footers were being let off much too lightly, but according to the plan they had made he leaned well out of the basket like the others, and tried to catch the cut lines which were still trailing from the Lead-Footers. He managed to grasp Lily's as she floated by, and he held it firmly, as though she were a hooked fish.

In a few minutes all the Lead-Footers had been captured in this way, and had been transferred to Leo's balloon. He held all the lines in his hand, with the Lead-Footers at the end, like someone holding a bunch of toy balloons. He steadied the basket over the huge oak tree near the tower and the Lead-Footers, scowling, had to follow him. Ben couldn't understand at first what Leo was going to do, but then he saw that Leo was tying the Lead-Footers, in a bunch, to the topmost branch of the gigantic tree. At once they tried to climb down, but became entangled in each others' lines. They started to fight and argue bad temperedly, struggling in the air.

"They won't get down for hours," said Leo cheerfully. "They'll never think of helping each other." As he spoke the lines became thoroughly knotted, as each Lead-Footer fought to be the first one free.

"Then they've got to climb down the tree," Leo went on. "I reckon they'll be ready for bed by that time."

Several hours later, a small balloon child sighed. "It was the very, very best Midsummer Night we ever had!"

The misty dawn was breaking and everything at the farm looked pale pink. Everyone was smiling and tired, but deliciously so, after the night's celebrations. In later years people often asked Ben and Miranda exactly what they did on that night. They could never remember clearly, but they knew that they had never been so happy.

"Well, we sailed and sailed," Miranda would say, her eyes dreamy.

"*Everywhere*, with no trouble at all," Ben would add.

"And of course we really *looked*—we saw all the other balloons."

"Yes, yellow ones, silver ones—all colors—the sky was full of them——"

"And we saw the most marvelous places——"

"And heard the funniest jokes——"

"We had the most wonderful time——"

Words always failed them at this point.

The night had ended in a huge party and banquet, at which everyone cooked a dish they had invented, and they played games on the grass.

"I do wish we could write down this menu," said Miranda, eating yet another delicious mouthful. "I bet we forget all these foods afterwards." She was right—they did.

Just then, his shirtfront pink as apple blossom in the dawn light, Pushkin stalked proudly out from the farmhouse. "I've invented a mar-r-vellous new dish!" he purred. "It r-really is super-r-r-b!" With a flourish, he whipped off the cover of his masterpiece. It was fish and chips!

Chapter 16

FLIGHT INTO THE SUN

"BUT how can you be sure the Lead-Footers are really, properly beaten?" Ben was asking. He and Leo were sitting on the grass one day later in summer, peeling potatoes. Ben thought idly how much he hated this task at home, and yet how delightful it seemed in the company of the Balloon People.

"Well," replied Leo, "I suppose they'll be back, but not for some time—no, I should say they won't bother us for a long while."

"I do wish we'd got rid of them for good," said Ben impatiently.

"That's *Their* kind of talk," said Leo. "I reckon there are too many of them, in any case." He tried to explain what he meant. "There'll always be plenty of Them around, but perhaps one day—well, you never know"—he looked up into the sky—"they might learn a few things. . . ." Ben could see from his face that he wasn't going to say any more.

"Swallows are gathering," said Leo, looking at the barn roof.

At that moment some of the balloon children came running. "Look what we've found!" cried one, holding out a handful of ripe blackberries for Leo to see.

173

Leo's face grew more thoughtful than ever.

Emma and Miranda came out into the sun. "Are those potatoes ready now?" asked Emma. "We're waiting for them and——" She stopped suddenly when she caught sight of the blackberries, and glanced at Leo quickly, who said nothing. "And we need some more wood for the fire," she added briskly, as though nothing were wrong.

"But the fire's banked up high already, Emma," said Miranda in surprise, "and it's no colder than yesterday."

"Oh yes, it is," said Emma emphatically, and went in.

The rest of the day passed as usual, though Ben and Miranda felt a difference somehow—it was hard to put one's finger on it. Something was in the air, but what? Later in the week Felix was standing, staring at the twittering swallows, now lined up thickly on the barn roof. Now and then one made a short trial flight. "They always do that just before they go," said Felix, with the same expression that Leo had worn earlier.

"Go?" said Miranda. Felix didn't reply.

Another day, soon afterwards, Emma took Ben and Miranda aside. "I've been meaning to ask you," she said kindly, "if you've got plenty of friends in Langleymere. Have you?"

"Well, of course we have some," began Miranda, "but——"

"Then that takes a big load off my mind," said

Emma. "And I hope you've got plenty to do at home this winter?"

"There's school, of course." Ben looked gloomy.

"Ah yes, school—I'd forgotten. Well, you'll be all right then." Emma began to lay the table to show that this was meant to be the end of the conversation.

Gradually the summer was drawing to a close. Miranda and Ben made regular visits home, of course, and lived happily in two worlds, but every so often a chill seemed to fall on the sunny farm. One day, Becky and Pushkin returned from market, and told everybody how all the corn in the district was now harvested. All the balloonists listened with great interest. Ben and Miranda felt left out.

Finally, they were all sitting outside one day, having tea under a large sycamore tree on a perfect, golden afternoon. There was a gust of wind and a few leaves blew off, falling onto the table. Miranda picked one up, thinking how pretty it was, red, orange and brown. The balloonists suddenly jumped to their feet, expressions of excitement and alarm on their faces. Pushkin snatched the leaf quite rudely from her and examined it closely. "It's later than we thought," he cried. "This settles it—it's an *autumn* leaf!"

Ben had heard enough. "What *is* the matter with you all?" he demanded. "You've all been so strange lately. I couldn't help noticing—the blackberries and the swallows—all that fuss about feeling colder, and the harvest being finished. What are you hiding from us? Haven't we a right to know?"

"Yes," said Leo, "you have a right, but we didn't know how to tell you."

"Tell us what?" asked Miranda.

"They're all signs, you see," said Emma gently. "The swallows leaving, the ripe blackberries and now the falling leaves—they're all signs of winter."

"Winter?"

"Don't you remember," Emma continued, "the times you've asked us what we did in winter?"

"You mean, about why you don't need winter clothes, and why you can't stand the cold—and that the children don't know what winter is?"

"Yes, those kind of things. Well, you see, they don't know what winter is because we're never here then. I know it must sound odd to you——"

"I remember now," said Ben, looking less puzzled. "On our first flight, Pushkin said something about your not being here in winter, and we did think it was strange, but he didn't seem to want to talk about it."

"No, that was because you weren't yet one of us," said Leo.

"So you're trying to say that you're—going away, is that it?" said Ben slowly.

"I'm afraid so," said Leo solemnly.

"But we're coming with you?" cried Miranda eagerly. Leo shook his head. Miranda looked unbelieving and then as though she would cry. "But you'll come back then?"

"We'll be back in the spring—like the birds," said Leo, beaming.

"What will happen to the farm and all your sheep?" asked Ben.

"We close up the farm for the winter and the sheep go to our neighbors across the hill," replied Leo.

"Now," said Mr. Perkins, his black eyes twinkling, "don't be sad. You are true balloonists now, each of you. You've proved it by your conduct in the battle —and before. We owe you a great debt."

Ben and Miranda looked at the ground, embarrassed. "Oh, I don't know about that——" began Ben.

"And so," continued Mr. Perkins, "we would like to give you a small present, to show our gratitude." He nodded to Emma, who went behind the tree and brought out a parcel.

"Open it, it's your pr-r-resent," yawned Pushkin.

Ben and Miranda took off the wrapping, and there was a balloon, beautifully made, about as big as an armchair.

"Sorry it couldn't be full-sized," said Leo, "but where would you keep it?"

They all laughed.

"Blow it up," said Emma.

"Why, it's beautiful," said Miranda. It was red and gold, an exact replica of the one they had first sailed in, and inside were models of all the equipment that had so fascinated them. There were even flowers in the basketwork boxes around the sides.

"This will be something to remember us by, while we're away," said Emma.

"Where will you go?" asked Ben.

"To the South," said Felix, smiling at the thought of it.

"To the South!" echoed the balloon children.

"And when do you go?" asked Miranda.

"Ah!" said Leo. "We've lingered too long already. We must fly to the sun."

"The sun!" cried the others.

Ben and Miranda were standing by the tower, which had played such an important part in their adventures. Autumn leaves now lay thickly around it, and Ben shivered, in spite of his sweater.

"There they are!" Miranda pointed into the distance.

The balloons, two of them, drew nearer. One was purple and gold, and the other was pink and orange. They were more splendid in the autumn sun than the colored leaves on the ground. Glowing brilliantly and swaying gently, they swung over the children's heads. Over the top of the gay geraniums in the flower boxes they recognized Pushkin, his fur richly gleaming, and Leo, his round face smiling. It was impossible to be sad, looking at those happy faces. Soon all the Balloon People were leaning out, waving and bouncing. One of the children bounced so high that Emma had to pull him back by his shirt.

The balloons circled widely, taking their bearings. Something fell out of one to the ground, but Miranda and Ben were too absorbed in the sky spectacle to notice it. They heard Pushkin's voice faintly, as the balloons swept round.

"The cock is crowing South!"

Then, slowly but surely, the balloons began to sail away. The autumn sun was going down in a mass of red fire, and gradually the balloons faded into the setting sun, looking rather like suns themselves. Miranda and Ben strained their eyes to catch a last glimpse, and then shut them, dazzled by the brightness. When they opened them the balloons were gone.

Ben's attention was then caught by the thing that had fallen out. It was a black bowler hat. Inside, on the band, they saw: 'Henry Perkins Esq.'

They turned to go home, Ben carrying the hat.

The summer was over, but there was the spring to look forward to.